MW00527839

CYCLED

GOLD HOCKEY #13

ELISE FABER

Cycled
BY ELISE FABER

Cycled
Copyright © 2021 Elise Faber
Print ISBN-13: 978-1-63749-034-1
Ebook ISBN-13: 978-1-63749-033-4
Cover Art by Jena Brignola

GOLD CAST OF CHARACTERS

HEROES AND HEROINES:

Brit Plantain (Blocked) — first female goalie in the NHL, loves boy bands

Stefan Barie (Blocked) — captain of the Gold

Sara Jetty (Backhand) — artist and figure skater

Mike Stewart (Backhand) —defenseman for the Gold, romance guru

Blane Hart (Boarding) — center for the Gold, number 22

Mandy Shallows (Boarding) — trainer and physical therapist

Max Montgomery (Benched) — defensemen for the Gold, giant nerd

Angelica Shallows (Benched) — engineer at RoboTech, also a giant nerd

Blue Anderson (Breakaway) — top forward in the league and for the Gold

Anna Hayes (Breakaway) — Max's former nanny, no relation to Kevin Hayes

Rebecca Stravokraus (Breakout) — Gold publicist, makes killer brownies, known at PR-Rebecca

Kevin Hayes (Breakout) — forward for the Gold, no relation to Anna Hayes

Rebecca Hallbright (Checked) — nutritionist for the Gold, plethora of delicious vegan recipes, known as Nutrionist-Rebecca

Gabe Carter (Checked) — doctor, head trainer for the Gold

Calle Stevens (Coasting) — assistant coach for the Gold, former national team member

Coop Armstrong (Coasting) — talented forward on the Gold, addicted to historical romance audiobooks

Mia Caldwell (Centered) — 5th degree black belt, brings the snark

Liam Williamson (Centered) — Gold forward finding his love for the game, charming and pushy in equal measures

Charlotte Harris (Charging) — new Gold GM, hates losing and the game Chubby Bunny

Logan Walker (Charging) — defensemen for the Gold, skills include: cockiness and being able to buy presents that make Charlotte squirm

Dani Eastbrook (Caged) — video coach for the Gold, tech nerd, could fix your computer in a flash, shy

Ethan Korhonen (Caged) — forward for the Gold, killer power play skills, known as Big Juicy Brain

Fanny Douglas (Crashed) — silver medalist, skating coach for the Gold

Brandon Cunningham (Crashed) — brown curls, penchant for hallways, Kaydon Lewis's agent

Kaydon Lewis (Cycled)— yummy stubble, great with kids, doesn't mind a little snot

Scarlett Andrews (Cycled)—quiet, perfectionist, resembled Bambi on ice

Devon Scott (Block & Tackle) — former player, current owner Prestige Media group

Becca Scott (Block & Tackle) — Devon's assistant

ADDITIONAL CHARACTERS:

Charlie Andrews — Scarlett's brother

Bernard — head coach

Richie — equipment manager

Dan Plantain — Brit's brother

Diane Barie — Stefan's mom

Pierre Barie — Stefan's dad, owner of the Gold

Spence — former goalie, married to Monique, daughter Mirabel

Monique — married to Spence, former model

Mirabel — daughter of Spence and Monique

Mitch — Sara's boss

Allison and Sean — Blane's parents

Pascal — Devon Scott's security lead

Roger Shallows — Mandy's dad

Grant and Megan — Devon's parents

CHAPTER ONE

Scarlett

SHE WAS BAMBI.

Remember that scene where the cute little deer was on the ice and his legs were going every which way?

That was Scar on ice.

Great, now she sounded like one of those old PSAs.

This is your brain on drugs.

This is Scar Andrews on ice.

A wail caught her attention, and she wobbled as she turned to the right, saw a little girl crying on the ice. But before Scar could make her very shaky way over to her, her friend Fanny all but sailed across the ice, pretty and graceful, even on a love-hazed cloud. Well, they couldn't all be graceful silver-medalist skaters now, could they?

Scar watched Fanny kneel and comfort the little girl, and in just a few seconds, they were both on their feet and back to class.

It would have been nice if Fanny had fallen for Scar's brother, Charlie, but it was pretty damned great that she'd fallen for Brandon.

Brandon, who was lovely and awesome and was currently working at a table in the corner of the rink, his laptop open, his earbuds in, papers spread out on the chair next to him. Even though he had a cushy corner office at Prestige Media Group, he preferred to bundle up and work where he could see the woman he loved.

And stare at Fanny, at his woman, with warm, love-filled eyes.

God.

Scar wanted *that*.

A man—someone, *anyone* to look at her and see something special, a treasure to them, even if the rest of the world didn't see it.

Her heart squeezed tight.

No. No, she didn't want that. She wanted to look at herself and see the treasure, the special, not to rely on another person to find it.

And anyway, she wanted to keep working. She was finally doing what she'd dreamed of, and as an assistant publicist for the Gold, her job was to manage the team's social media and do her best to keep the public loving them.

That part wasn't hard.

The guys were great.

As great as Brandon was.

Ugh.

"Ms. Scar?"

She blinked, forcing her eyes away from Brandon and his obvious affection for Fanny, and looking down at the tiny boy at her knees. "Hey, Dominic. Everything okay?"

His bottom lip wobbled.

Oh shit.

"Hey, buddy," she said, clumsily getting to her knees. "Talk to me."

That lip kept wobbling and was now joined by tears.

Fuck.

"Candace said that I'm bad at skating," he sobbed.

All the kids were bad at skating. That's why she—equally as bad, or perhaps maybe marginally better, depending on who was judging—was helping with the class. She wasn't good enough at skating to help any other time.

Front and back.

Slow turns.

Doing her best to not eat shit.

And mostly she succeeded.

Unfortunately, she couldn't tell him they were all terrible.

"You're doing really good, buddy," she said. "You're just learning, and I know you'll be good in no time."

The tears were still there, but they were slowing. "Really?" he said, snot trailing under his nose.

"Really," she said, shuddering. She started to pull a packet of tissues out of her pocket, kept there for exactly this reason, but before she could get one out, someone else skated over.

Someone tall and handsome, who had her in a constant battle to keep her panties up and around her hips.

They just wanted to drop right off anytime Kaydon was around.

He had arms that made her drool, a strong jaw with a hint of stubble she wanted trailing over her skin, and lips that would pillow perfectly against hers.

If only they didn't work together.

She liked this job.

She *loved* this job.

Which meant she wanted to keep it.

And while the Gold were a treasure trove of couples working together and living out their happy endings, Scar didn't have that track record.

When she was in a relationship, things never went well.

And that unwell transitioned into her life, her job, her happiness.

She had terrible taste in men, and when those relationships

ended, her shit got dive-bombed. She lost her job. She got kicked out of her apartment. She was dogged by debt collectors, or psycho ex-girlfriends she hadn't known existed (or were wives, in one case—and not the ex-variety—and the reason the man she'd been dating had become *her* ex), or mothers who were pissed that the wedding they'd been planning without Scar's permission (or their son's, for that matter) was off.

So, suffice to say, she was on a break from men.

It was work and friends and rebuilding her life.

No. Men.

Unfortunately, one look at Kaydon when he'd joined the team had made her want to reconsider her hiatus. It was more than his glorious jaw and yummy stubble, his deep brown skin and sexy body. He was nice and talented and was…just a really decent guy.

Case in point?

That exact moment.

Kaydon bent next to her and scooped up Dominic. He said something that made Dom laugh, and he didn't seem to care when Dom rubbed his snotty nose against his shoulder.

His big hand came to the back of Dom's helmet, and then he took off with the little boy in his arms, zigging and zagging through the cones, avoiding the other kids effortlessly. Dom laughed and held on and by the time they circled back, both man and boy had huge smiles on their faces.

A moment later, Dom's skates were on the ice, Kay holding him steady as he spoke quietly.

Scar still couldn't make out the words, could only watch Dom nod intently before he threw his arms around Kaydon's neck and hugged the huge hockey player. And—oh sweet baby Jesus—her ovaries, because Kaydon didn't hesitate, just hugged him back and patted him lightly on the helmet before lightly pushing him forward so he could rejoin the other kids. Scar could barely resist the urge to clamp her hands to her heart and sigh, the longing to know him better was so intense.

Used to shoving that longing down—she'd done it for nearly an entire season—she pushed to her feet and continued to patrol the ice, making sure everyone was happy and tear-free and staying far, far away from Kaydon, lest he see that longing.

Lest he have any longing of his own—wishful thinking, she knew, but she was decent looking, smart, and had a nice body, so a woman could dream...even about sexy hockey players—and decide he wanted her. If that ever happened, she knew that she would crumple like a house of cards or a cheap suitcase or...

Thank God—for her ovaries, that was—Fanny blew the whistle, stopping her simile searching, and the session of classes was over.

Scar's feet ached—skates were *not* for the faint of heart—but she started cleaning up the ice anyway so Fan didn't have to, attempting to *not* notice that Kaydon was picking up cones much more rapidly than she was.

And moving closer to her and her bumbling self.

"I can get this, you know?" he rumbled, skating past her, graceful as fuck, a pile of cones in his arms.

Much bigger than the pile she'd managed to collect.

"I know, but I like to..." She trailed off.

Because he couldn't hear her, not when he was already on the other side of the ice.

The rink had cleared out, the kids having moved into the lobby to change, and Brandon and Fanny were in deep discussion over something at his makeshift workstation. Scar lumbered toward the door to the ice, her cones the worst sort of Jenga tower, and managed to just barely climb up the step to get off the ice as Kaydon returned from stashing his stack of supplies around the corner.

"Let me," he began, reaching for her cones.

She walked right by him.

"Okay," he muttered.

She ignored him. It was much better for her sanity, for her

hiatus from men, for her disaster of a relationship wake that would follow in her tracks if she *didn't* brush by him.

But apparently, today, he was done with Scar not paying attention to him. "What's your problem?" he snapped, following her into the narrow hallway.

"I don't know what you're talking about," she said, gracelessly bending so she could place the cones on the stack.

She mostly succeeded.

Mostly because a few tumbled off and scattered on the ground. Stifling a curse, she knelt and started picking them up.

So did Kaydon.

Fucking hell. She was trying to be *good*.

Why did he have to help her, even when he was clearly pissed?

"Scarlett."

Cones. *Cones!* Focus on the flipping cones.

After snagging one, she set it on the stack, but because she wasn't paying attention, that setting resulting in her knocking over the entire pile, and the cones went *everywhere*.

Shit.

She reached for them, hands flailing, trying to shift around carefully since she was still wearing skates. Last thing she wanted to do was slice off hers or Kaydon's fingers, since he was too damned nice and *still* helping her. Two cones to the left. One by his ankle. Another just behind the stack. One more just out of reach.

"*Scarlett*."

A warning this time.

Glancing down, she realized exactly where that *just out of reach* cone was—or rather what she was *reaching* for.

His dick.

Well, she was reaching for the cone that was less than an inch from his dick.

Eek!

She froze, but before she could pull back, his fingers encircled her wrist.

Warm and a little rough.

Her lips parted on an exhale, and she shivered.

"Scarlett," he said again, and this time his voice was like his fingers, warm and a little rough.

She wobbled.

He shifted a little closer, smoothing a lock of her hair off her cheek. "Why don't you like me, Scar?"

Still processing all that warm and rough *and* him smoothing back her hair, it took her a second to process his question. But the moment she did, she unstuck, laughter bubbling up her throat and filling the air.

He let her laugh for a minute before his hand—the one not tracing light and lovely circles on her wrist—reached up and cupped her cheek. "I don't love being on the butt end of a joke, baby."

That stoppered up her guffawing.

His thumb moved, swiped at the skin beneath her eyes, and she realized that she'd been laughing so hard, she had tears on her cheeks.

"You're not a joke, Kaydon," she whispered.

He was so far away from that it wasn't even funny. *She* was the joke. She was the one who was trying to be good.

She was the one who was going to fail.

Again.

Because she leaned forward, whispered before he could reply, "It's not that I don't like you, Kay. It's that you are the sexiest man I've ever seen."

And then she kissed him.

CHAPTER TWO

Kaydon

WELL.

This was fucking awkward.

Scarlett in his arms. Her mouth on his.

Her tongue—okay, *that* part wasn't awkward. *None* of her parts were awkward. They were lush and overflowing his palms, and her ass was…well frankly, it was a lesson in perfection. It was just that the woman he thought hated him was *kissing* him.

And, okay, maybe that wasn't the most awkward part.

Because the kiss was pretty fucking great.

His knee twinging as she crawled her way into his lap? Uncomfortable, and maybe a little awkward, mostly because it was clumsy and he scrambled to keep hold of her, and he hated that he still had pain even after all the time and energy he'd spent rehabbing his injury.

Her skates being damned close to his femoral artery?

Now *that* was awkward…and dangerous.

So, while he wanted to pull Scarlett closer, explore this kiss that was fucking fantastic, or maybe even to strip her naked and kiss every inch of those curves, he had to push her away instead.

Her eyes were glazed. Her lips swollen. She reached for him again, breathed, "More," against his lips.

"Stop, Scar," he ordered.

And yeah, maybe it was a little sharp.

But fuck, those blades on her feet were lethally sharp…and damned close to his cock.

One second, glazed eyes and a pretty flush on her cheeks.

The next, the glaze disappeared, and her face went red. Bright red. Fire engine red. It clashed with her freckles, with her copper-colored hair, and he wondered how far it went. Down her neck? Across her chest? Farther? Dipping down between those gorgeous breasts.

She started to scramble off his lap, legs and arms flying as she tried to find her feet…and nearly unmanned him.

"Fuck!"

Scarlett froze at the curse. "I—*I*—" She stumbled back a step, knocking over the cones, almost eating shit.

"Scar," he began, hopping to his feet, grabbing for her arm.

She yanked away from him.

Her glasses had slipped down her nose, and she pushed them up with her pointer finger in an absent movement he'd seen her do a hundred times before. Only this time, he was close enough to see what the tattoo was on the inside of that finger.

A little bee.

Complete with stripes and wings and a tiny stinger.

Why?

Just because it was cute—though, the small insect looked fierce rather than cute? Or because it held another meaning, a deeper one?

"I'm sorry," she said, and the statement was shaky as fuck.

Shaky enough to pull him out of pondering that bee and back onto her face.

His eyes would have to not be working for him to miss the hurt there. Fuck. "Scar," he said, reaching for her again.

Another skitter backward. "I'm sorry," she said. "I'm—" A shake of her head, that red hair flying everywhere. She spun and started running—or trying to, anyway. Because she made it all of a foot before her skate got hooked on the edge of the black mat that was laid over the concrete to protect the blades from being dulled on the floor.

And she went down.

Hard.

He tried to reach for her.

But he wasn't fast enough.

Her knees collided with the concrete with a *crack* that made him wince. Fuck, she was going to be feeling that tomorrow. *Fuck*, she was going to be feeling that *now*.

She rolled over, and he saw that her sweats—the tight black sweats that lovingly cupped her ass, an ass that had been tempting him all night—had torn. Blood was dripping down her knee, a bruise already forming.

"Scar," he murmured, kneeling down next to her.

She scooted away from him, tried to get to her feet again. He already knew that was dangerous, so he gripped her ankles, pinned them in place, and went to work on her laces. She was still for a moment, then tried to jerk them free.

"Stop," he ordered.

She didn't.

He didn't either. Just continued unlacing the skates, loosening them enough that he could slide one off then the other. Then her sock-covered feet were free, and he was tossing the skates to the side. Apples. Her socks were covered in dancing cartoon apples with cute little smiles, holding watering cans. That had rainbows pouring out of the spouts.

Adorable.

Just like her.

"Apples," he murmured.

She yanked her foot back, stood, and promptly winced. But even as he got to his own feet, she tucked that wince away and lifted her chin, slid away from him. "I'm sorry," she said again. "I shouldn't have done that. I was—I—" A tear slipped out from behind her glasses, dripped down her cheek. "Please, don't get me fired. I won't—I won't ever do it again."

He was still processing the apology when the rest of the words processed. "Fired?"

The red on her cheeks somehow grew. "I—it was wrong. Please, accept my apol—*oh!*"

Kaydon had heard enough of her apologizing. So, he scooped her up into his arms, carried her back toward the ref room where he and the other guys normally got their skates on. He, for one, didn't mind interacting with the kids while they were getting ready for these sessions of Fanny's they volunteered at. The kids were awesome. However, the parents—especially the divorced single ones—sometimes got a little dicey.

It had been decided it was easier for the Gold players to get ready in the back and then proceed directly to the ice.

He thought it was a little overkill.

But he also wasn't the one who'd gotten his ass pinched.

So, he went with it.

Today, he was just relieved that he was the last one off the ice—and the last one to get changed.

Because that back room was empty.

He slammed the door behind them, flicked the lock, and carried Scarlett over to the bench, plunking her onto the metal surface.

"What are you doing?" she whispered.

Kaydon didn't answer, just stood and retrieved the first aid kit that was secured by the door. Then he knelt at her feet, glance sliding up those apple-printed socks, those shapely legs encased in black Lycra, and stopping at the injury on her knee.

Kit on the bench next to Scarlett.

Opened and some supplies at the ready.

He pushed the torn material to the side, swiped at the cut on her knee with one of the cleaning pads.

She hissed out a breath.

Kay blew lightly on the injury, hearing her hiss again, and one look at her eyes told him that the hiss wasn't from pain, not that time. It was the same reason his heart was still pounding in his chest. The same reason his fingers itched to touch her, his mouth watered to taste her.

Heat.

It *burned* between them.

He resisted the urges, smoothing a bandage over her cut. Then he grabbed his sweatshirt from the hook, rolled it, and tucked it under her knee, elevating it a little bit more.

The ice pack from the first aid kit set gently on top.

"So," he said, sitting next to her, bending over to untie his skates, "you don't hate me."

Scar choked, her body jerking, her glasses sliding down her nose.

He leaned over, slid them up. "And you kiss like sin."

Her lips parted, and for a moment, he thought she was going to stay silent. But her chin came up again, and her words were firm. "That was a mistake." She grabbed the ice pack, plunked it onto the bench.

Not missing a beat, he reached up, put it back on her injured knee.

"I—"

"Not a mistake," he said, taking a turn at firm.

She scoffed. "So says the man who practically shoved me out of his lap."

"So says the man who pushed you—and those deadly blades strapped to your feet—away from my cock." And his femoral artery.

Not that he was thinking much about bleeding out at that moment—or at least not blood in *that* sense. Blood moving toward his dick? Yeah. *That* was on his mind.

The flush in her cheeks had been receding.

His words made it flare again.

She pushed her glasses up her nose before she turned away. "I'm sorry," she whispered. "I didn't know."

"I know," he said. "And I don't care."

That had the benefit of getting her startling blue eyes back on his. "You *don't* care that I nearly chopped your dick off?"

He smiled. "Put it that way, and I'd rather keep it where it is." He bit back a groan when her eyes dipped to his crotch, to where his cock was still at half-mast from that taste of Scarlett, from the pink on her cheeks. "For the record, I don't mind you near my dick. I'd just rather keep the sharp blades well away from it."

"Right." Her gaze slid away, and he watched her neck work as she swallowed. "Well"—she removed the ice pack again, this time setting it on the far side of her body (and out of his reach) —"I should go."

"Scar—"

She popped to her feet and started for the door.

He shoved off his second skate, moved after her, reaching her just as her hand wrapped around the handle. Ass to his crotch. Her scent in his nose. Her nape—bared by the ponytail her hair was pulled up into—exposed and calling to his mouth, his fingers.

Her fingers spasmed on the handle.

He covered them, bent to murmur in her ear. "Come out to dinner with me?"

Statue.

She'd gone so still she could have become one.

Then slowly—*slowly*—she shook her head, her ponytail brushing along his jaw, catching on the stubble he couldn't be bothered to shave.

"I can't," she whispered.

He gave in to the urge to touch his lips to her nape, to inhale the soft scent of woman, of flowers and vanilla, floral and sweet and all too tempting.

Her body softened.

His tongue flicked out, tasted that vanilla, and suddenly he was craving cookies, having a vision of baking them with this woman, wrapping his arms around her to "help" her mix the batter, leaning close and repeating the kiss as they scooped them out onto the tray, watching her steal a warm cookie and joining in on the thieving then "punishing" her by smearing melted chocolate on her nose and kissing it off. And then smearing it on other parts and—

She shifted closer.

Kaydon cut off the fantasy—and yes, it was quite a well-rounded fantasy. Yeah, he liked baking. Not that he admitted it to too many people, and certainly not to his teammates. He'd already gotten enough shit since earning the nickname Kitten, and he didn't need any more flak from the guys. Well, they probably wouldn't, because they were decent dudes, but he definitely wouldn't put it past them to show up on his porch and expect him to bake them an apple pie or something if they found out that he spent his free time baking shit.

Which so wasn't the point of this.

The point of this *being* that this was the first time he'd culti-vated a daydream involving baked goods.

Daydreaming about women? Yes.

About this beautiful, curvy redhead currently between him and the door? Definitely. Too many times to count.

But making double chocolate chip cookies with this beau-tiful woman? No. He could honestly say that it had never crossed his mind.

It was damned sure going to now.

Double chocolate chip cookies.

Peanut butter brownies.

Zucchini bread with slivered almonds.

Homemade ice cream with hot fudge from scratch.

Okay, the last would be the best fantasy—and hopefully something that might become reality if he could convince her to go to dinner with him, or better yet, to come over on a Cheat Day. Plus, it made for easier licking and came without the risk of salmonella.

"Come out with me tomorrow," he said softly.

All the softness left her body, and she straightened, trying to move away from him. But since the door was in front of her and he was behind her and she wasn't asking him to back off, she didn't get very far.

"I can't," she said again.

"Why?"

Her shoulders rose and fell on a sigh. Her forehead dropped forward against the wood of the door. "Kaydon," she began and sighed again as she lifted her head and glanced at him over her shoulder. "I just *can't*."

God what he wouldn't give for her to be looking at him over shoulder while they were both naked, while he was pounding into her, and—

There was a knock at the door.

The handle turned.

Or tried to, anyway, since he had locked it.

"Scar—"

She moved with a speed that surprised him, arching her body back, bumping him away from her in an action that could have taken place on the ice. A sharp check, causing Kaydon to lose his footing and stumble back.

Scar flicked the lock and tugged open the door so quickly that it nearly swung wide and cracked him in the face.

Fanny was on the other side.

Her expression went from love-struck and slightly harried—a product of her fiancé and teaching classes to under twelves all day, respectively—to concerned. "Scar?" she asked, a frown drawing her brows together. "Why was the door locked?"

Scar spoke, and it was so effortless, so easy-breezy and unaffected that Kaydon might have believed it was the truth if he hadn't just had his body pressed to hers. "Oh, it wasn't locked," she said, smiling widely and as she waved a hand toward the knob. "I think I was just trying to turn it at the same time you were."

Fanny's frown deepened.

"Well anyway, I'm off," she said, breezing by Fanny. "I'll catch up with you two soon!"

Then she was gone.

Fanny glanced at him. "What's up with that, Kitten?"

Kaydon stifled his groan at the nickname. There was no getting rid of it, he knew that much already. Then he stifled his urge to chase after Scarlett and corner her until she agreed to go out with him. Instead, he shrugged and said, "*That* is Scarlett. If anyone could somehow manage to lock us in here without actually locking us in, it would be her."

Fanny laughed. "That much is true. I don't know how so much disaster always follows in her wake, but it does."

Disaster.

Hmm.

Maybe her *"I can't"* was because she was worried that things would go wrong between them?

That was a legitimate concern.

Fanny made her way to her locker and started taking off her skates, chattering his ear off as he put on his shoes, shrugged into his Gold hoodie. They talked about the kids and how they were progressing, and he got roped into another session the next week.

Though *roped in* was a loose description for it.

He liked hanging with the kids.

Plus, Scarlett was volunteering at the same time.

He smiled before exchanging goodbyes and heading into the hall. Yeah, he liked Scarlett Andrews. She was beautiful, smart, trailed by disasters, sweet as hell.

And kissed like a goddess.

Now how to convince her to give him a shot?

His gaze caught on something just before he turned to leave the hallway.

A glint of silver. Pink laces and black eyelets.

Kaydon smiled.

CHAPTER THREE

Scar

"WHERE ARE THEY?" she muttered, digging through the trunk of her car. She always left her skates in her trunk. Because she only used them for these sessions with Fanny and the kids.

It wasn't like she was hitting up a public skating session just for fun.

Probably, that would be a good idea.

She might stop resembling Bambi if she actually practiced.

But...alas...she didn't really like skating that much. Feeling like she was part of something, helping out a friend, being with the guys on the team who had become her family more than her actual family—*that* was what had gotten her out on the ice the first few times.

It also helped to get pointers from professional hockey players and figure skaters.

Helped her not to eat shit...most of the time, anyway.

None of that, however, helped her find her skates in the mess of her trunk. Why—*why!*—wasn't she more organized? She could pull together a press conference, draft a statement from management or players, curate Instagram and TikTok content like a champ.

But she couldn't keep her car clean.

What was wrong with her?

Her mom would say so many things—so *so* many things—were wrong with Scar, not the least of which was going by a name that represented a blemish on someone's skin.

Scar—who preferred to go by Scar because it was one small thing she could control, because it was one small thing that her mother couldn't—thought of it differently.

Less blemish and more representation of strength and surviving and old pain buried deep.

Unfortunately, her lack of keeping her car clean skills or not, she had a sinking feeling where her skates were...or at least where they had been last week. Where Kaydon had taken them off and flung them to the side in the hallway.

Groaning, she dropped her chin to her chest. "Why, Scar?" she whispered. "Why?"

She already knew the why.

Because she was a mess who'd been thinking about that kiss with Kaydon, her mind spinning with all the reasons why she should have accepted that dinner date...and all the reasons she was glad she couldn't have.

"I love my job," she whispered. "I don't need anything else—"

"Even if the skate fits?"

The voice made her jump and—

"*Ow!*" she exclaimed, rubbing the top of her head before turning to see Kaydon standing there.

That explained the heat prickling on her nape.

She had just figured it was because she was thinking about Kaydon and his strong legs and his stubble and the deep brown of his eyes that reminded her of the thick, creamy hot chocolate that Molly's made from scratch for each and every person who ordered it.

Not that powdered crap with hot water.

And certainly not Hershey's syrup in regular milk like her grandma used to make her—not that she'd turn that down. One, the nostalgia was strong with that type. Two, she didn't discriminate against chocolate of any variety.

She definitely had preferences, though.

The dark chocolate of Kaydon's eyes was high up on her list of all-time favorites.

And they were focused on her, making her stomach go all fluttery, her palms sweaty, and her lips tingly. What she wouldn't *give* to accept that dinner invitation.

She could.

So easily.

Just say yes, and it would be done.

But—she forced her gaze away from Kaydon's—she also knew how it would end. An unpalatable memory for him. Disaster for her.

And she really loved her job.

She couldn't lose it.

Not again. Not when Rebecca had taken a chance on her. Her boss was reducing her hours so that she could spend more time with her new baby—an adorable little girl named Kayla... who already had more shoes than any baby could ever wear.

So fitting.

But a little sad that a tiny human whose age was still counted in months had more—and fancier—shoes than Scar.

She didn't have the sharp dressing thing down. Hell, she didn't have fashion sense of any sort. Scar was much more likely to be found in a Gold pullover and jeans, her feet clad in comfy sneakers. Because foot comfort was important...and also because she hadn't had a day working for the Gold where she had walked less than fifteen thousand steps.

And she sure as shit wasn't doing that in heels like Rebecca did.

A warm hand settled on the top of her head, fingertips

massaging gently. "Shit, Scar, baby, you okay? I didn't mean to scare you."

So gentle.

So soft.

His fingers. His *voice*.

She found her gaze going toward his, being drawn in like a tractor beam, diving deep into the chocolate depths, swimming in a chocolate pool like a character from *Charlie and the Chocolate Factory*. Found her lips parting and words tumbling off her tongue as she had an out-of-body experience and heard herself saying, "I want to drink your eyes like they're the tastiest milkshake."

What. The. *Fuck?*

Scar jerked when what she'd said processed, lurching away from him as nausea crashed through her like a fucking tsunami. Slammed into the shore, debris slicing through her, currents yanking her from side to side.

Oh God.

She was going to puke.

I want to drink your eyes like they're the tastiest milkshake.

Time to throw herself off a cliff. *Now.*

"Hey," he said. "Hey. What's the matter?"

She whirled, started to dart away—maybe to hide in the rink, maybe to go and find that cliff—but Kaydon caught her, slowly spun her to face him.

"Sweetcheeks, what's the matter?"

Her eyes went wide. *"What's* the matter?" How could he seriously be asking her that?

A flash of white. A glimpse of that sexy smile hidden amongst his stubble. "Is this about the milkshake thing?"

Duh. How could it possibly be about anything else?

He seemed to hear her thoughts—or in all likelihood, he could read everything crossing over her face. Everyone always said she wore every single emotion and worry on her face.

"I've been thinking a lot about chocolate where you're involved," he murmured.

Her eyes flared. "Um…"

"In case that's not clear, sweetcheeks," he said, leaning close, his hand sliding into her hair again, massaging her scalp, "I've been thinking about licking it off all those curves."

She gaped at him.

"Also, I've thought about swimming in your eyes."

She jerked again, nearly whacked her head on the trunk again—albeit the edge of it rather than the bottom of the opened compartment, but Kaydon slid his hand around, shielding the side of her head and then shifting her back so he could use his other hand to close the metal covering.

It *thunked* shut.

His palm came to her cheek, thumb sweeping over the skin just beneath one eye and then the other. "I've never seen eyes the color of yours. So blue. So clear. It's like looking into the waters of the Caribbean."

She shivered.

Who talked like that?

Kaydon did apparently.

And it should have been cheesy—and she supposed it was—but it was *her* cheesy—

No. *No.* This wasn't *her* anything. Except, even as she was thinking that her body drifted closer to his, and his fingers brushed along her nape. "Come to dinner with me."

God, that would be *awesome.*

Except…then it wouldn't.

She sighed, stepped back, shivering when his fingers drifted along her skin before falling away. "I can't, Kaydon. I'm a disaster. My life…it's *always* a disaster and—and—" God. How could she possibly explain the fuckery that was her past? "I promise you," she said. "I'm trying to do you a favor here. Relationships with me never go well, and I don't want to…I *won't* do that to you."

She held his gaze when he looked like he was going to protest, but she—despite her best intentions—found herself shifting forward, her body moving close to him. Stay. She wanted to stay there. Well, she wanted to do so much more than that, but—

Scar sighed.

Stopped herself from dropping her head and resting it against his chest. Stopped herself from wishing that she wasn't a total mess, that she wouldn't spill that mess all throughout her life, throughout the organization she so loved working for when it all inevitably imploded.

She was in public relations.

God, the *multitude* of ways this could go wrong.

"Sweetcheeks," he murmured.

Her breath slid out of her, and that endearment had her placing a palm on his chest, resting it lightly over muscles she wished she would be able to give herself permission to explore.

"Please, stop pushing this," she whispered. "Every time you're nice to me and touch me and tell me sweet things about my eyes, it only makes it harder for me to tell you no."

He stared at her for a long moment.

Kept those solemn brown eyes on hers.

He stepped back.

She lost those muscles, the steady thrum of his heart beneath her palm, but kept the solemn brown eyes.

Scar braced herself for him to agree with her.

Readied herself for the blow.

"Good."

She blinked. "What?"

Kaydon bent, picked up the skates—*her* skates—that had somehow ended up near her back tire, and handed them to her. "Good," he repeated.

"I—*what?*"

He rubbed his nose against hers. "Good," he said for a third time. "See you on the ice, sweetcheeks."

And then he was gone, striding away, his ass lovingly

caressed by pale gray sweatpants—and *fuck,* the man had a great ass.

She blew out a breath, watched him—*and that great ass*—disappear into the rink.

Then stood there, the cool morning air coating her skin, the parking lot starting to fill up with cars and families and kids getting ready for their skating classes.

"Hi, Ms. Scar!" A little girl—Claire—called. She had on a bright purple skating dress, pink gloves, and her hair was pulled up into ponytails, one tied with a fuzzy purple scrunchie, the other secured with a bright pink fuzzy tie.

"Hey, Claire!" she called back, forcing herself to smile and wave at the little girl as she took off for the rink.

Cool morning air.

The smell of fall in her nose.

The imprint of Kaydon's touch on her skin.

And her brain full of wondering what the hell *Good* meant.

"I'm in *so* much fucking trouble," she whispered.

CHAPTER FOUR

Kaydon

SHE WAS KLUTZIER THAN NORMAL.

He knew it was because of him, knew he should probably feel bad to have her so discombobulated. But instead, he could only watch the show. She was fucking adorable, all legs and arms and horribly bad at skating.

It was admirable, actually.

To see how little she improved, even though she had basically been getting private lessons for months from a silver medalist figure skater who had made it her job to perfect the skating skills of professional hockey players and whose side gig was to run a company that put on skating classes—classes that taught hundreds of kids every week how to skate.

But, it was also admirable how she continued to come out and help—basically with wrangling the kids and making sure they stayed in their respective sections, being the official Kleenex provider (since kids and snotty noses went hand-in-hand, but kids and being on the ice and snotty noses went even *more* hand-in-hand), and taking attendance. She was here, stumbling around on her skates, helping with boo-boos, making sure the kids were in the right place, and too fucking cute.

He'd lusted after her since the moment he'd seen her.

Then had spent the rest of the season feeling stung when she avoided him. Now summer was winding down. The new season was a few weeks away, and...she liked him.

And...he had plenty of time on his hands.

He smiled, mentally rubbed his hands together.

She wobbled, and he was moving before he thought about it, skating over to her, steadying her by putting his hands on her waist—yeah, maybe a little lower than was prudent, but though she started, she didn't stiffen, didn't pull away.

In fact, she melted against him.

"Okay," he murmured, bending to speak into her ear, inhaling the soft scent of her.

"I—" Her hips canted slightly, brushing against his crotch.

Now *that* he liked.

But *that* he couldn't have at the moment. Kay couldn't be running around with a hard-on, not in these sweats, not on the ice surrounded by kids.

He shifted his hips away from her, pressed a kiss to her neck. "Bend your knees more, sweetcheeks."

"Kaydon," she gasped, whipping around to face him.

He steadied her by gripping her shoulders. "What?"

"You can't say *that!*" Her gaze darted from side to side.

Frowning, he rewound to what he said...and then he smiled. "What are *you* thinking about?" he murmured, brushing his thumb along her jaw. "I just meant"—he bent and tapped the side of her knees—"to bend these so that you'll be steadier."

"I—oh—I—"

"But if you want to get *on* your knees," he said softly as he straightened, "I wouldn't turn you down."

Her cheeks went red.

"I'd even return the favor."

More red. Her tongue slid out to taste her bottom lip.

God, he wished they weren't on the ice right now.

Then again, she probably wouldn't have let him get this close if they weren't. Especially after her earlier statement. So, even though he couldn't do everything he wanted—i.e., pull Scarlett into a shadowed corner and kiss her until she agreed to go on a date with him—he was glad to have this moment with her.

"Bent knees," he murmured.

Her eyes flew to his.

"Beautiful eyes." He tugged a lock of her hair, made sure she was steady…and then skated back to the group of kids he was helping to herd.

A crunch.

A rush of air.

"Do I need to give you a talking to about my friend?"

Fanny. The woman in charge. The woman whose fiancé was Kaydon's agent—Brandon—who was so smitten with her that he'd convinced Kaydon to help with these classes in the first place.

"Did I give Brandon a talking to?" he asked, righting a kiddo before she could hit the ice.

"Yes," she said without preamble. "I seem to remember him telling me that you had some stern words for him."

Well, shit.

Now that she mentioned that…

He made a face. "Why don't you just get the talking to out of the way then?"

She smiled, and it was really fucking smug. "Oh, no, Kitten," she said, patting his arm. "I'll just save that for a future date."

"Fanny—" he began.

"I'm sure I'll need it," she called over her shoulder as she skated away from him.

"Fan—"

She stopped.

"Mr. Kaydon!" A pair of tiny arms slid around his legs.

Fanny grinned, waved one finger at him, and skated off.

Smothering a sigh, he glanced down at the little girl hanging around his knees. "What's up, Little Bit?"

"My *name* is Claire."

He scooped her up, the ice from her skate blades dripping onto his shirt and soaking through the fabric. He'd shucked his jacket earlier and would probably be missing the waterproof material in a few minutes when he put Little Bit down and was dealing with a wet T-shirt in a cold rink (and not working hard enough to break a sweat).

But now?

With Claire throwing her arms around his neck and squeezing tight, asking—loudly—into his ear, "Make me fly, Mr. Kaydon!"

"What was that, Little Bit?" he pretended to clean out his ear. "I couldn't quite hear you."

"My *name* is Cla—*ah!*"

He took off, holding her tightly against him. Her twin ponytails flew through the air, trailing like streamers as he zoomed them through the rink. Fast enough to make her squeal, but not fast enough to be dangerous with the multitude of obstacles—kids, cones, teachers, tires, *more* kids—littering the ice.

Just as quickly, he returned Claire to her class.

And then he helped with some actual teaching, coaxing a few kids into taking their first tentative strides—without a stack of buckets to help them stay upright—coaching another little boy to do some backward swizzles.

"Toe to heel," he said, moving backward across the ice, "toe to heel, Ty. That's it!" Kaydon stayed by Ty's side for a bit, doing the movement with him, praising Ty when he did each skill, feeling pride well up in him when the little boy—small for his age of six—managed to connect three of them in a row. "Nice job, bud!"

They fist-bumped.

Ty turned around and started swizzling in the other direction.

Kaydon went in search of another kiddo to help, teaching crossovers and a hockey stop, avoiding any skill that required a toe pick—since his skates didn't have one. He'd leave Fanny and her pack of paid fancy-toe-pick-using teachers to take care of those, and his volunteering ass would get to do the fun stuff.

Like more zooming.

This time with Dominic.

And then Rylie. And Samantha and Tony and Ellie.

And each time he returned a kid from zooming back to their station, he would glance up and see Scarlett staring at him—or at his ass, or at his crotch.

And each time he caught her looking, he winked at her.

Watched her cheeks go redder.

Watched her lips part and her eyes darken and—

He winked as he zipped past her, carrying a giggling Thomas, grinned when she stumbled and jerked, barely keeping her balance.

And Kay knew that he'd be getting that talking to from Fanny sooner rather than later.

Fine by him.

CHAPTER FIVE

Scar

OKAY, so she was a coward.

She'd snuck off the ice while he'd been in the middle of helping one of the kids do crossovers—a hellish lesson in balance that she'd never mastered.

Probably because she'd never mastered even basic skating.

Either way, instead of helping out by cleaning the ice like she normally did, she skipped out five minutes early, practically tore off her fingernails loosening her laces, and then shoved her feet into her boots.

At least she didn't run out of the rink to her car in her socked feet like last time.

She'd had to come back the next day—the worst sort of morning after—and search through the lost and found in order to find her UGGs. They were expensive as hell, but the comfiest shoes she'd ever had the pleasure of putting her feet into.

Like walking on clouds.

She wasn't going to let her boots get lost.

Even if it meant the equivalent of dumpster diving through

a load of dirty socks, mismatched shoes, and loads and loads of gloves—none of which actually formed a pair, of course.

But even with all her nail-breaking and attempt at subterfuge, anyone want to guess who was standing next to the driver's side of her car?

Looking too fucking handsome and completely relaxed.

Even though she felt like she'd run a marathon, and her feet were sweating in her cloud-like boots. Hell, she was sweaty in a *lot* of places, not the least of which were her feet.

"Kaydon," she sighed. "I told you I can't—"

"You forgot these," he murmured, holding out her gloves.

She'd taken them off to tackle her laces.

And now she couldn't even get mad at the man. Because he was being nice and returning her things and—*sigh*. Seriously, she needed to start keeping better track of her belongings.

"Thanks," she whispered.

"I'm not going to ask you to dinner," he began, and she went stiff, her shoulders tightening. Here they went. He was going to tell her she was too much trouble. "But know that the invitation is open at any time."

"Right." Another whisper.

Because that shouldn't be a trickle of disappointment coursing through her. It shouldn't! But it was anyway, and... how stupid was that?

And seriously, Andrews. Get it *together*.

Fingers on her jaw. "I'll see you soon," he murmured.

She swallowed.

He leaned in. "Unless you want to see more of me now?"

Yes. Yes. All of you! I want to see all of you. Right. Now.

Scar shook her head.

"Bye, sweetcheeks."

Then he was gone, and all she wanted to do was to call him back.

"And that would be stupid, Scar," she muttered, unlocking her car and plunking her skates *and gloves* into the back seat.

"Because you finally got him to leave you alone. And that's what you wanted, right?" She slammed the rear door, opened the driver's side one and plunked down into it. "Right," she whispered. "That's what I want."

Grabbing the handle, she yanked her door shut, shoved the key into the ignition.

And turned it.

And...nothing happened.

Just a quiet *click* and nothing that sounded remotely like her engine turning over.

She tried again. *Click.*

Again. *Click.*

Fuck. Why was this her life?

Maybe the key was broken? She pulled it out of the ignition and put it back in, knowing that it wouldn't solve the problem but too set on her desperation for this to not be her life, so she was going with it. She turned the key again.

Click.

Click. Click. Click. Click—

Knock-knock.

She screeched, jumping in her seat, clamping a hand to her chest, and turning her head to glance out her window.

Two guesses who it was?

She cracked the door.

"Problem?" Kaydon asked, his big fingers wrapping around the top of the door and tugging it open. He rounded the edge, crouched in the opening. "What's up, sweetcheeks?"

Silently, she turned the key again.

Click.

"Starter," he murmured. "You got Triple A?"

She shook her head.

"I got you." He stood and closed the door, and she had only a moment to wonder if him "having her" meant that he was going to leave her in the parking lot with a car that didn't work —and she could definitely say that wouldn't be the worst thing one of the men she'd dated had done to her. But he didn't keep her guessing for long. Instead, he rounded the hood of her car, opened the passenger side door, and sat down next to her. "I'd offer to try and fix it," he said, "but trust me. You don't want me under there."

"A man who admits his own shortcomings?" she asked. "I don't believe it."

His smile filled the interior of the car.

With puppy dogs and rainbows and cotton candy.

Yes, she was delirious.

Yes, she still half-expected a golden retriever puppy to mysteriously appear in her back seat. Or maybe ten of them. With wagging tails and colorful collars and names like Fluffy, Cutie Pie, and Kitten (yes, that was a silly name for a dog, but then again, she had a thing for Kaydon—as in she couldn't stop thinking about him, and since his nickname was Kitten...well, there she went).

No golden retrievers appeared.

But Kaydon *did* put his phone up to his ear and start talking to an operator, apparently from AAA, explaining what was going on with her car, and requesting a tow truck. "It'll be an hour," he said as he hung up. "Come on."

He got out of the car, slammed the door.

Before she could blink, he was at hers, tugging it open, unbuckling the seat belt she didn't remember buckling, and pulling her out from the car. "What are you—?"

"They're going to call me when the tow truck is close."

Which didn't explain why he was tugging her away from her car, shutting the driver's side door, snagging her keys from her hands, and bleeping the locks. He drew her through the parking lot, out onto the sidewalk, and—

"Is this where you take me to easily dispose of my body?"

He froze.

And then something wonderful happened.

His laughter filled the air, wrapping around her like a fuzzy, warm sweater, warming her slowly from the outside in, sinking into her skin, bubbling through her blood…injecting itself straight into her heart.

Thump-thump.

Thump-thump.

Thump-thump.

"No, sweetcheeks," he murmured. "I'm bribing you." Her brows drew together. "With tacos." He turned her body so she could see a tiny glass door leading to a literal—

"Hole in the Wall?" she asked.

It was kitschy—the door surrounded by faux sheetrock and two-by-fours and what literally looked to be a half-finished wall.

"What is this place?"

Kaydon pushed open the door, tilted his head toward the opening. "Why don't you go inside and find out?"

———

"THESE ARE AMAZING!" she exclaimed, though really, it was more like mumbled since she said it through a giant bite of taco.

Soft corn tortillas. Cool, crisp bits of cabbage. Shredded pork. Crumbled cheese. A sauce that was just spicy enough for her to break out in a sweat. Kaydon really *was* bribing her with tacos. Hell, she'd already had three of them and was thinking about having three more.

And that was with an already full stomach.

And three margaritas.

And…somehow, she was having dinner with Kaydon, even though she'd promised herself she wouldn't. Well, if it could be considered dinner when they were stuffing their faces at two o'clock in the afternoon. Speaking of which…

"Aren't you on a special diet or something?" she said around her next bite.

"Hmm?" he asked, his eyes on hers, but his focus definitely on his own taco.

"Don't you have to follow the famous Nutritionist Rebecca's meal plan, just like the rest of the guys?"

He took another bite—demolished half of what she thought was his fourth taco—and then shrugged in a movement that was casual, but drew her eyes to his in a way that was totally *not* causal, mostly because then she was drooling over his shoulders (yummy, built), and then his arms (biceps a woman would kill to hang on to...at any time, but particularly while he pounded into her), and then because the man had a body built like sin, every other part of him she could see (which were some really good parts, but also, not the *best* parts since his ass, thighs, and—it had to be said—dick were hidden beneath the table) made her fingers itch to touch him.

"Don't follow the diet in the summer," he said around his next bite.

It should be gross—that he was talking and chewing—but since she was doing the same, she figured two chewers made a right.

"During the season," he said, picking up his next taco. Another shrug that showed off that coiled strength. "Yes, I'm really strict, and a few weeks before as well to ramp up my conditioning. But I'm a little looser during my off time...which means"—he swallowed, glanced at his watch—"I'm going to pretend today is a Cheat Day and get my taco on." He winked.

She nearly choked on *her* taco.

And then, of course, her *other* taco decided to perk up and pay attention, to sizzle with need that resembled the hot sauce burning the back of her tongue.

His brow came up. "So many thoughts swirling through that gorgeous brain of yours."

Gorgeous brain.

It shouldn't sound like anything that resembled a compliment. Brains weren't gorgeous. She supposed they looked rather gross, if she were forced to describe one, not that brains were typically an object she described.

"So many dirty thoughts I want to hear every single detail of."

"I—"

He reached across the table and swiped his thumb over her mouth.

Her lips parted on a gasp.

"You had a little…sauce," he murmured.

"I—"

"Scar?"

"What?"

He nudged her plate of tacos closer. "Don't overthink it, sweetcheeks," he said. "Just enjoy the tacos and"—he reached over, swiped his thumb again—"*that* was because I've been dreaming of this mouth since the first moment I saw it."

"I—"

"Eat, baby."

One more nudge of her plate closer to her before he picked up another taco and started eating.

She was at a dinner she'd promised herself she wouldn't attend.

Sitting across from a man she'd vowed to keep her distance from.

Falling when she'd sworn she wouldn't.

And all she could think was that he had an amazing smile.

Fucked.

Scar was absolutely, totally fucked.

CHAPTER SIX

Kaydon

SOMEONE WAS LOOKING out for him, he decided.

First the car.

Then the tacos.

Now...*this*.

The tow truck driver saying he could take Scarlett's car straight to the dealership for repairs, since Scar had a ride home, and now Kaydon had the opportunity for a captive audience.

"I really couldn't impose," she was saying, "I'm sure you're busy and have things to do and—"

"Not an imposition if I offer, sweetcheeks," he said, thanking the tow truck driver and guiding her to his car. "Plus, you've had three margaritas. I think it's better if I drive you."

Red on her cheeks. A lighter flush than the one she wore when she was embarrassed, just a hint of pink grazing the skin just beneath her eyes, drifting closer to her nose, reddening the cute, upturned tip of it.

That space called for a kiss, and he found himself unable to resist, bending to press his mouth to the spot, just for a heartbeat.

"Kay," she whispered.

"Buckle up," he murmured, gently pushing her down into the passenger's seat of his car then stowing the bag she'd shoved some things from her trunk into, along with her purse, into the back seat.

He heard the belt *click* as he opened his own door and sat down. Then did up his own, pulled out of the spot, and started driving.

"Directions."

Her eyes were closed, her head resting back against the seat. "Hmm?"

His mouth curved into a smile. Three margaritas. Six tacos. He couldn't lie and say he wasn't impressed by both of those numbers, couldn't lie and say he didn't enjoy the glimpse of her face relaxed and soft. Would she look like that first thing in the morning, her hair fanned out on his pillow?

He hoped that he would get the opportunity to find out.

"Can you give me directions to your place, Scarlett?" he asked.

"Don't call me that."

The words were slightly sharp.

"What?"

Her eyes slid open, and he glanced over at them, saw a trace of something in their azure depths he couldn't completely decipher, but if he had to guess, he'd say that *something* looked like pain. "Sorry," she whispered. "I just...I just prefer that people call me Scar."

"Okay."

A blink.

As though surprised he'd agreed so easily. That prickled the back of his mind, wove itself in with the other tidbits he'd picked up about her over the last months. Jumpy, shy, but always ready to volunteer her time, eager to help out, to be part of the team.

He didn't think she'd ever missed a team activity, at least not one that he'd gone to—and he usually went to them all.

But she was jumpy and shy and didn't like her full name.

And there was that glimpse of pain.

Hmm.

He didn't know who'd hurt her, but he was going to find out, going to make them pay. Kaydon inwardly rolled his eyes, knowing that he sounded like a bad movie villain, even as the sentiment remained. He didn't like the idea of her being hurt, wanted to go full alpha at just the thought of her stubbing her toe on the couch.

He'd throw that damned thing out just for being in her way.

And then maybe light it on fire, tear the stuffing out of the cushions, rip off the legs.

"So, Scar," he murmured, not acknowledging that glimpse of pain. There would be time for that later. Now, he needed to focus on continuing to build her trust.

"Yeah?" she whispered.

"Directions to your place?"

She startled slightly. "Right." And then she gave him her address, the exit to take off the freeway. It wasn't far from his place. Maybe three miles, and he had to wonder how he'd never run by her house. Probably because she lived in a smaller community of newer houses and he lived up the hill in an older, more established (read: expensive) one, and while running down the hill should have been easier than hauling his tired ass back up it, the reality was that his knee injury had made jogging downhill challenging...and it fucked with him for several days afterward.

Not worth it.

Not worth the pain, the limp.

Now, however, it might be. Mostly because he was envisioning Scar waiting at the bottom of the hill, her kissable lips turning up in greeting when she saw him.

He'd limp for days just to have that smile directed at him.

"Did you always want to be in publicity?" he asked as he navigated his way to her place.

Her eyes found his, held for a brief moment before he had to glance back at the road that had his heart skipping a beat, his pulse skittering, his palms itching to touch, his lips desperate to kiss her, to taste her, to feel the slick dart of her tongue against his, her nails biting into his shoulders, and the fantasy was so real for a moment that he almost didn't hear her question.

"Did you always want to be a hockey player?"

She wanted to know something about him.

Sure, it was clearly a deflection, a question-for-a-question avoidance technique to avoid sharing anything personal as she sidestepped answering *his* question. But she wanted to know about him, and that made his chest puff up (mentally, not literally since that would look fucking weird while he was driving), so he gave it all to her.

To win this woman, he wouldn't be able to hold anything back.

She'd been hurt. She didn't trust others easily, and even though she bent over backward for everyone else, she didn't expect the same in return. Scar didn't expect people to go out of their way for *her*. Well, fuck that. It was decided. He was going to be that person for her.

"Yeah," he said and shot her a grin, "I always wanted to be a hockey player. I once got a game-used stick, and my parents swore that I slept with it like a teddy bear for years."

"Your parents swore?" she teased. "Or you actually did that?"

Another grin. "Either. Both."

She giggled. "Well, it must have done something for your skills, you *were* the number one draft pick."

"Kind of like sleeping on my history book taught me about the Revolutionary War?"

Laughter—a full belly laugh that gave Kaydon that chest-puff feeling again—filled the car, and he laughed with her when she gasped out, "Just absorbed right through your skin into your brain." A breath. "Damn, if only I'd used that technique for Calculus. I would have been a doctor."

He tugged a lock of her hair. "Or a rocket scientist."

More chuckles and, fuck if he didn't feel better making her laugh and smile than he had when he'd gotten picked in the first round.

That had been filled with nerves and anxiety, hopes pinned on him that felt increasingly heavy.

And so much pressure.

Pressure that had made it difficult to enjoy the moment, pressure that hadn't gone away, pressure that had been exacerbated by the coaches of his former team—so much so that he had played through an injury when he shouldn't have, practiced extra during his recovery when he should have been resting, and generally fucked up his knee for the rest of his life.

Funny story, hockey players needed their knees to play.

They kind of helped with skating and turning and keeping one's balance.

"Do you still have the stick?" she asked once she'd gotten herself under control.

He nodded. "Yeah."

"That's really cool," she said, and her voice grew quiet, "I don't have anything like that from my childhood."

"No?"

A pause, and he glanced at her out of the corner of his eye, watched her stiff shoulders relax and held his breath, wondering if she would give him something, give him some insight into her. "No," she murmured, "I don't. My parents…"

He waited.

"Well, let's just say that I've been a constant source of disappointment my whole life." Her gaze drifted out the window, and she fell silent for long enough that he was running through subjects in his mind, trying to find one that would bring her smile back when she added, "It was easy to throw my stuff away." A breath, her voice going even quieter. "Easy to throw *me* away."

CHAPTER SEVEN

Scar

FUCK.

Why had she said that?

Seriously—God, *seriously*—*why* had she said that?

She kept a lid on that shit for a reason. She didn't want it to define her, didn't want it to drag her down again. Scar had moved beyond it, started over, built her own life with her own rules and expectations and happiness.

She had her happiness, too.

Without anyone else.

Found deep within herself.

Not reliant on *anyone* else. Just her. Just Scar.

But now she'd blurted out something that was kept beneath that lid, the memories she didn't like to dwell on because they did *no fucking good,* and she probably looked like the biggest idiot on the planet, getting all blubbery and teary-eyed after a couple of margaritas and a car that wouldn't start, still moaning and groaning about her mediocre childhood. "I'm—"

"Want to see it?"

She blinked. "What?"

"Do you want to see my stick?"

Her brows rose—and God help her—her eyes flicked down to his groin.

He cleared his throat. "Um—" And his ochre-colored skin took on the barest hint of pink. "That is—I mean, the *game-used* stick that I slept with...um...was *given* as a child. I live just up the hill off of Oak Tree and..."

They were almost to her house.

She was in a car with a man she was supposed to be avoiding.

The smart thing would be to turn him down, to continue onto her place, to end this before it went any further.

But...she couldn't.

There was something vulnerable about that slight blush, about the stammering over sticks and sleeping with them...and the light touches on her jaw, the little tugs on her hair (which should be annoying, but somehow made her smile), and the way he seemed to see her—the messy, klutzy, unorganized parts of her—and not care.

That was what had her saying, "Yes."

"I'm not trying to make you come over to my place..." he was saying—or rambling, really, and that had her settling further into the feeling, holding tightly on to it.

"Yes," she repeated.

"I just thought that maybe—" He stopped, glanced over at her (luckily, they were stopped at a signal). "Yes?" he whispered.

"Yes," she said, nodding, her lips tipping up, "I'd like to see your stick."

He paused, repeated. "Yes?"

She giggled, nudged his shoulder. "Did I break you?" she teased. "Should you drop me off at home just in case? I don't want to go plowing into a milk truck. Imagine the mess that'll make."

"I'm into messy things," he murmured, and the slight

roughness to his voice had her shivering (and then biting back a smile when he reached forward without commenting—or missing a beat—and turned on the heater). "I've got you held captive. No way in hell am I letting you go now."

She turned to him, said slowly, "Why are you so good at saying creepy things?"

Russet eyes gleaming with mischief on hers. "Why are you so good at fucking up my game?"

"I—" She started to form a joke—something along the lines of his best game being acting like a sociopath, which probably really wasn't all that funny, all things considered—when the other meaning of his words sank in.

What if he *wasn't* joking?

What if she *really* was good at messing up his game? And what if the game she was messing up wasn't just his ability to drop a really good line, and what if it was his work, what if by game he meant hockey, what if—

A thumb running along the edge of her jaw. "What's going through that beautiful brain of yours?"

There he went again, complimenting her brain—and seriously, *who* did that? But more than the compliment, her brain wasn't beautiful. It was a fucked-up place to reside, chaos creating, easily spiraling. It struggled to contain and bury painful memories, somehow attracted men who were vengeful, who loved that chaos, who enjoyed taking a ride on that Tilt-a-Whirl.

Except Kaydon.

Well, the Kaydon she thought she knew.

The Kaydon who was smart and insightful and sweet and… she stifled a sigh. Because she really hoped the Kaydon she thought she knew was the man who Kaydon really was.

He didn't seem to thrive on her chaos and spiral. He extended a hand and tugged her back onto the roller coaster, strapped her in until she made it through to the other side.

And what?

It had been all of two interactions.

Except, that wasn't fair.

Because it wasn't just two interactions.

He'd been on the team for a season and change, and she'd never seen him act like a jerk to anyone. And she was around a lot. Unseen a lot. Not ignored, but a common enough sight that the guys didn't tend to act like they were on their best behavior —didn't have "guest manners"—as Rebecca called them. Meaning there were penis and fart jokes, plenty of ribbing, and copious use of the F word. The shine was gone. The teasing was on point. But—also a Rebecca mention—these presented the best opportunities for candids.

The practical jokes hit on TikTok.

The photographs worked well on Instagram.

She, thankfully, wasn't in charge of Twitter. She didn't have enough of a quick wit to be successful in that avenue. Snark wasn't something she had in spades—at least not enough to be funny on the Big T.

And good God, what was she doing calling it the Big T?

Who did that?

"Scar?"

Blinking, she asked, "Hmm?"

A brush of fingers along her cheek. "What are you thinking?"

She was in that state of mental spiraling—her thoughts spinning around and around and thinking about absolutely nothing useful—so she answered without thinking, "That I shouldn't call Twitter the Big T."

Silence.

Then laughter, laugher that filled her up and held her tight in the best sort of hug. His hand dropped onto her thigh, just above her knee, and she had to hold herself very still in order to not hitch it higher, to not squirm against the hold and "accidentally" brush that lovely, big hand against all the parts of her that were desperate for all the parts of him.

"What else?" he pressed.

"Hmm?" she murmured again, still studying that big hand. He had a scar across the back of it, faint pink lines that criss-crossed and spoke of an old surgery.

What had happened? Did it still bother him?

"I know you weren't thinking about Twitter," he said. "Or at least, not *only* Twitter," he added, pausing briefly at the gate entrance to the Oak Tree community. Seemingly not thinking about it, he reached up to the visor and pressed a remote and the large metal gate swung open slowly.

So fancy.

"Scar?"

"Yeah," she said, deliberately keeping her eyes on the houses as they wound their way through the community.

Now *talk* about fancy. She could work her whole life and not even dream about being able to afford one of these homes.

Well, then again, she wasn't a professional hockey player now, was she?

"What were you thinking that made you look sad?"

A mom was pushing a stroller.

A couple was walking hand-in-hand.

A man was washing his car.

All normal activities. All little stab wounds that reminded her of what she'd never had. A mom to hold her hand. A dad to wash the family car.

Normality.

"I don't want to fuck up your life," she whispered. "I'm..." She sighed and admitted the truth. "I'm really good at that, and I like you, Kaydon. I don't want you to hate me because I mess up your game, whether that's hockey or—or—"

He pulled into the driveway of a house.

A house that wasn't hers—easily spotted because not only had they driven past her neighborhood, but it was much nicer than hers with a gorgeous stone exterior, a large front porch, a path that wove through flower-filled planter beds, and a lovely mahogany garage door with oil-rubbed bronze finishes and windows in the top panel. She'd priced one of those doors when she'd moved into her place, and since she was a single woman with a single woman's salary who was incredibly house poor after buying a property in the expensive Bay Area market, she'd about choked on her own spit when the estimate had come back in.

Hence, the old door she currently still had.

And if it had to be unlocked by hand and yanked up with all her strength, then so be it.

Hell, she'd considered it her equivalent of kettlebell exercises for the last six months.

Her arms had never been this toned.

A thumb ghosting across her bottom lip, Kaydon's beautiful brown eyes on hers. "You're not going to mess up my game. Not on the ice," he said, leaning close, his spicy, bright scent surrounding her, "not off it. I'd need to *have* game for the last, and I'm far from the smoothest guy on the block—"

She started to protest.

He cupped her cheek. "My nickname is Kitten, sweetcheeks," he said, his lips turned up at the corners. "I promise you. I don't have a lot of game. In fact, I basically have *no* game. So, there's nothing for you to screw up on that front."

"But—"

"And more than that, when I'm on the ice having someone to play for makes me play better."

She'd had a protest on the tip of her tongue, some handy excuse to put him off, to gain some distance.

But she couldn't argue with that.

Or at least, she couldn't summon up an argument.

So…she just said, "Oh."

To which Kaydon smiled, bopped her on the tip of her nose, and said, "Yeah. *Oh.*"

CHAPTER EIGHT

Kaydon

HE HAD HER BACK.

At least for the moment.

Forcing himself to lean away from her, lest he kiss that soft look off her face, Kaydon pulled on his door handle, got out of the driver's seat, then rounded the hood just in time to help Scar out of the car.

Not that she needed the help.

But it was an excuse to keep touching her, even as he played at being polite.

"Thanks," she murmured, when he tugged her up.

He brushed his lips across the back of her hand in answer then released her and grabbed her things out of the back seat. She didn't comment on him snagging them, which was a minor miracle because she certainly didn't need her skates inside his house. But he wanted them inside, wanted her things in his house, wanted that connection.

Even *if* it was just her purse and random things she'd shoved into a bag from the trunk of her car.

He wanted them.

Wanted *her*.

So, he was hauling them into his house...and dragging her along, too.

Knowing he was grinning like a fool, he weaved their fingers together and drew her up to the front door.

Her eyes were on the garage. "Why don't you park inside?" she asked as they walked up the two steps and he stuck his key in the lock.

"Door's broken," he said, letting them in.

For some reason that made her laugh, and then her laughter dissolved into awe as she made her way down the hall. "Wow, no *way*," she breathed, and for a second, he thought she was fawning over the wood floor (a typical response for the uniquely striated material) or the open staircase that led to the second story (the second most common compliment). But she didn't so much as glance at either of them, nor the kitchen, or the painting that hung beneath the stairs—a bright abstract piece that his mother had bought for him.

Instead, Scar went right to the bookcase tucked down the hall.

Except, it wasn't just a bookcase.

And she seemed to know that.

"No *way*," she said again.

"It's *Game of Thrones*," he said, coming up behind her after he'd set her skates, bag, and purse on the bench by the front door (another gift from his mother).

Her hand went to the book and started to tug, but not in the right direction, and not with enough force. Which meant, of course, that he had to step closer—darn—and had to reach around her in order to show her how the hidden handle worked.

A tug of the spine.

The latch inside the hidden door popped open.

He moved forward—darn again, somehow that movement brought him close to Scar's back, brought her scent into his

nose, her body into his arms—as they stepped into the hidden
library. The door had cost a ridiculous amount of money considering it was all of three feet wide and eight feet tall. If he broke
down how much he'd spent by inch—as he'd done when he'd
gritted his teeth and written the check to pay for it—he had to
fight back nausea, and he could have sworn that he'd broken
out with hives.

It wasn't a house, wasn't a new car (though spending money
on an expensive sedan had *literally* made him break out in
hives, so much so that he'd left one dealership and gone next to
door to a cheaper one, ending up with a mid-priced car that
served him just fine and he didn't care if someone dinged his
door in the grocery store parking lot).

But he'd bit the bullet and paid for the door.

Because the one thing he'd dreamed about as a kid—the one
thing aside from making it in the NHL—was that he wanted a
secret place of his own, somewhere to hide and get lost in and
to just let the stories flow over him.

Reading was an escape.

Had *always* been an escape.

In a four-bedroom house with six kids, two parents, two
dogs, and a cat, there hadn't been too many places to hide out,
to find a slice of privacy, to just be able to sit and read unin-
terrupted.

Now he had a house that was too big for him by far because
he wanted his family to have space when they visited, but he
had this room for *him.*

Because it was his escape hatch.

"Oh my God," Scar breathed, moving into the small library.
The walls were covered in shelves from floor to ceiling, each
one lit with soft inlaid lighting. A ladder moved on a track
around the space, more for aesthetics than actual use since he
didn't have much trouble reaching the top shelves, but the
object that took up the most space in the room was a huge
reading chair.

Round with edges that extended far enough forward to hold his body securely on the surface, loaded with pillows, covered in a fuzzy fabric that was soft and cozy and upon which he'd fallen asleep more times than he could count.

A light snaked up and over one of those long arms.

The other side had an adjustable tray with cupholders.

Blankets folded and tossed over the back. A basket with more pillows and blankets—another gift from his mom because she'd given him his love of books and knew what was needed in a cozy reading nook. She'd always tried to find ways for Kaydon to get a bit of privacy when his siblings overwhelmed him, even when she didn't have privacy herself. Because she understood how important it was. So, he'd made this space for himself, but…he'd also made it for her.

For her to have that same space and privacy when she visited.

Because he had the means to give it to her (and because she'd refused to allow him to pay for a nook in her own house).

And because she was amazing and deserved it, even if it was only here.

"I've never seen anything like this"—a shake of her head—"well, I mean I've seen it on Pinterest, but not in real life. It's… beautiful, Kaydon," she breathed, spinning to face him. "Like, seriously, gorgeous."

"I know."

She turned and smiled at him.

"But I have to give credit where credit is due," he said. "And that credit goes to my designer and my mother." A beat. "Who were one and the same. Though I did pick the chair."

She moved closer to him and for a moment, he thought that she was going to walk into his arms, to demand he hold and kiss her (and yes, he knew that was a fantasy because… patience), but then she shifted at the last minute and moved to the shelves. "And who picked the books?"

"Me," he said, and turned so he could slip an arm around

her waist, mentally fist-pumping when she leaned into him instead of pulling away.

Maybe it was the margaritas.

Maybe she was just getting more comfortable around him.

Either way, he didn't care.

He was just taking the victory.

"What about this shelf?" she asked, of course arrowing in on the one section of the bookcase that his mom had filled, declaring that, "Everyone needed a little happiness."

"My mom," he said.

"So not *all* you then." A grin, her eyes teasing, her glasses sliding down her nose.

He gently pushed them up.

Felt the hitch in her breathing as it drifted across his skin. "Not all me," he murmured.

"Kay?"

He dropped his head, dragged his nose along her throat, across her jaw, and up behind her ear, whispered, "Yeah?"

"Why do you have erotica on your shelf?"

"I—" He reared back. "*What?*"

Grinning, she bent and plucked one of the books his mother had left there. "This one is about dragon shifters and it's hot as hell." Another. "This one is a male-male-female, and the scenes are hot as fuck. Bondage. Anal"—her cheeks flared—"and double penetration." One more. "This one is a standard contemporary romance, but there is a scene where they're in a car and—"

He placed his fingers over her mouth. "Please, don't talk about my mom and anal sex."

A wicked gleam slid into her eyes. "But double penetration is okay?"

Shuddering, he moved closer, plucking the books out of her hands, and shoving them back onto the shelf he was going to pretend didn't exist—because if he acknowledged it, he might bring a flamethrower in and level this entire space, and then where would his peace be? "None of those things are okay."

"Hmm." She bent again.

He shifted behind her, ran a hand lightly down her spine—yes, he was a dirty old man, but seriously, the best way to run bleach through his brain was to focus on the sexy woman in front of him. Not a hardship at all. Especially when she glanced over her shoulder and smiled at him, slowly straightened until her back was against his chest, and he was able to wrap his arms around her. Also, not a hardship.

Vanilla and flowers in his nose.

Soft curves flush to him.

Fucking nirvana.

"You read that stuff?" he murmured.

"If by *stuff* you mean romance novels, then yes, I read them," she said, relaxing against him, not seeming to be opposed to him running his hands lightly up and down her arms, her torso. "Also, your mom has really good taste."

He clenched his teeth, gritted out, "Sweetcheeks."

"What?"

"Please, for the love of God, don't talk about my mom when your ass is rubbing against my cock."

She froze.

Her ass, which had been gloriously cushioning his cock, shifted away, and he muffled a groan. But she only bent again, picked up a book, and flipped open to a page. "This is one of my favorite scenes." Spinning, pulling out of his arms, she held it up to his face and ordered, "Read."

He followed that order, felt his mouth drop open.

It was...fucking hot, and he immediately inserted Scar into the heroine's role, himself into the hero's.

His cock twitched.

His hands ached to touch her again.

His words were hoarse.

"I thought you were shy."

CHAPTER NINE

Scar

"SHY DOESN'T MEAN DEAD," she murmured, her cheeks heating, her fingers tightening on the book.

She went to shove it back onto the shelf, but he grabbed her wrist. "Wait."

"What?" she snapped.

Why had she gone on and on about the books?

God, she'd talked about double penetration and *anal* and his mom. *Fuck.* What the hell was wrong with her?

"Keep that one out," he said, shifting behind her.

He was warm and hard and smelled like temptation. His voice was a velvet rasp, drifting over her breasts, her stomach, dipping down between her legs. It was a tongue sliding up her thigh, delving into the liquid heat of her pussy. She wanted to melt against him. She *wanted* to fuck him right on that oversized chair.

And meanwhile, she'd been talking about bondage and MMF and DP and butt stuff. She might as well have brought up nipple clamps and shibari.

"I'm—"

Lips on her ear. "If that's an apology, then I don't want hear it." He nipped her lobe. "What I *do* want to hear is your favorite book."

"Wh-what?"

Another nip, and then he spun her, turned her so fast she stumbled and ended up plastered against his chest. His palm came to her cheek, holding her face so that she couldn't look away. "I want you to tell me your favorite book," he murmured.

"Why?"

He pushed her glasses up. "Because I like to read, and I want to read something you like."

What planet was this man from?

"Then what?"

"Then maybe we'll act out something from one of them."

Said so silkily that it took her a moment to process that. And when she did, two different waves of heat flowed through her. One arrowed straight to her pussy then flowed outward. It had her breasts and her vagina doing a happy dance of epic proportions because they both really liked that one. The other was the crippling heat of embarrassment—because he knew that *she* knew about all those dirty things because she'd said his mom had good taste in smut.

Because she *wanted* to act something—everything—out with this man.

Sex. Life. More.

A relationship. A future built.

More kisses. More touches. More of Kaydon wanting to know things about her.

More…

Just *more.*

She was tired of fighting that more, tired of trying to lock everything down.

So…maybe this would all implode. Maybe this would end up being just another in a long line of disappointments in her life. Maybe, when it was all over, she would decide this hadn't been worth it. Maybe…

She needed to stop worrying and just live.

Damn the consequences.

"Kay?"

His voice was husky. "Yeah, sweetcheeks?"

"Will you kiss—"

Her phone blared from the hallway.

And not just any ringtone.

Her *mother's* ringtone. And seriously, she didn't need her mother's shit. Not right at that moment. Not ever. Not—

His palm came to her jaw, fingers lightly grazing her skin. "Ignore it."

How? How the fuck did one ignore that the Wicked Witch of the West was calling? How did she ignore that her mother was going to call and tear her apart and make her feel like shit and…Scar would let her?

Just let her.

She shook her head. "I—"

"Where do you want me to kiss you?" Kaydon asked, his pointer finger tracing along her cheek. "Here?"

"I…um…"

He rubbed his nose across her forehead. "Or here?"

"Kay—"

His thumb brushed over her bottom lip. *"Here?"*

Yes! She wanted his mouth slanting over hers, his tongue delving deep. She wanted to find a rhythm in kissing him that mirrored what she might be able to have with him in bed. She wanted *him,* tongue-fucking, real-fucking, finger-fucking, *every* type of fucking.

The ringing cut off.

The vise on her lungs loosened, and she leaned into him. Fuck, the man was gorgeous, and he smelled like the most intoxicating cologne she'd ever had the privilege of having in her nose. Ridiculous, yes, but she still wanted to be a cat in that moment, to rub her face against his, to imprint her scent onto him, his scent onto her.

"Scar?" Another brush of his thumb over her lips. "Here, baby?"

"Yes," she whispered. "*There.*"

His eyes changed, going molten. They were gorgeous with striations of gold and dark chocolate, the barest hint of amber, and it was hard to not stare. Scar fell into his gaze when she wasn't usually comfortable staring deeply into someone else's eyes—her modus operandus was a quick glance then shifting her eyes away. An assessment to see where she stood, to see if she needed to do damage control, to shore the situation up because she'd somehow fucked up, to shield herself from whatever barbs were going to be lobbed her way. Then hiding her own eyes so they couldn't see the turmoil inside her.

But with Kaydon, she looked. She was caught in that tractor beam stare, in that swirling brown and gold and amber, not missing the heat, nor the desire he didn't bother to hide. He wanted her, and there wasn't any derision in that.

Nor any disappointment.

Nor—

He leaned in, close enough that his breath was hot on her mouth. Puffs that had her lips parting, her tongue darting out to moisten the bottom one.

A soft groan rumbled from his chest.

She rose on tiptoe.

Her tongue darted out again.

Another rumble, his lips coming even nearer. "Scar," he whispered.

Her breasts brushed his chest as she shifted inexorably closer, drawn into him like she was a planet and he was a black hole. Time slowing, inching, *crawling* along until Scar felt like she was going to die if he didn't *just put his mouth on hers*.

"Sweetcheeks," he murmured, his mouth now so close that

the words caused their lips to brush, to intertwine and lock. His tongue flicked out, touched the tip of hers.

She melted—

Her cell phone blared again.

Jerking, their mouths mashed together, their teeth clicking. Pain radiated down her jaw and her nose. Kaydon cursed softly, leaned back, though his arms were still taut around her. Scar's head was spinning, her gaze unfocused. When it eventually cleared enough to see, Scar watched a drop of blood drip down the outside of his bottom lip. Her stomach churned, and bile burned the back of her throat. Even when she was trying to ignore the inevitability of impending disaster, she still created smaller ones in her wake.

Making him bleed by trying to kiss him.

Talking about DP and anal and his mom.

This was a mistake.

She pulled out of his hold, started to turn away, intending to go to her phone and to quietly, *gently* silence it—even if she felt like throwing it out the front door and convincing Kaydon to back his car over it...repeatedly. But she was an adult, dammit, and phones were expensive, and she couldn't afford to buy a new one, not if she wanted to afford her fancy new garage door (or a new car...or to *repair* her old one) sometime in the next century.

"What are you doing?" he asked, coming up behind her and wrapping his arms around her, his chin resting on her shoulder, his scent surrounding her.

"I'm going to shut off my phone."

"No"—a nip to her throat—"not the phone. What are you doing? In your head? What's happening in there that's taking you away from me?"

"I—" Words failed her. Again. And she fucking hated it. Fucking just wanted to be able to spit it out and just tell him. But it was *so* hard to make herself vulnerable in that way, to open herself up and spit it out.

Her phone rang again.

And that rage coiling in her, winding tighter and tighter, locking down her lungs, boiling through her blood, simmering just beneath the surface of her skin…finally exploded.

"I want you!" she yelled. "I fucking want you, and it's going to be a disaster. And I'm a mess, and my head will *not* shut the fuck up so I can for one fucking second enjoy something." God, her brain was so goddamned annoying. She was tired of the spiraling, of the mental gymnastics. For once in her life, why couldn't she just *not* be a disappointment?

"Want help?" he asked softly.

"I—" Realizing she was still yelling, she stopped, blinking at him. "What?"

"Want help getting your brain to shut up?"

Her cell shut off.

"I—"

Immediately began ringing again.

"Scar?"

"Yeah."

"Yeah, like you're answering me? Or yeah, because you want help?"

Ring-ring. Ring-ring. And fuck, her mother just did *not* give up, did she?

"Sweetcheeks," he murmured, pressing close to her again, his hand wrapping around the side of her neck. His eyes were bright, delving deep into hers.

And she couldn't *not* answer.

"Help," she whispered.

A nod. Then his hand dropped, and he stepped away, sending her stomach plummeting all over again.

Because he was leaving.

He was gone, disappearing into the hall and leaving her alone.

Well, she'd fucked that one up. Even when she plucked up

the courage to jump in, to ask for what she needed, she didn't get what she wanted, what she so desperately craved.

And great. Now she felt like crying.

What a big old drama queen she was.

Sighing, she took one last look at the gorgeous library, the hidden bookshelf door, tucking the memory safely away because this would probably be her first and last visit.

Right.

Better now than later. Better—

"Fuck, Scar," she whispered to herself. "Enough fucking spiraling. Shut up and move on and—"

She stepped into the hallway, stopped dead to see Kaydon standing there, one hand holding a bottle of tequila and the other two shot glasses.

"You got work tomorrow?"

"What?"

"Are you *working* tomorrow?" he asked.

Mutely, she shook her head.

"Good." He wrapped the arm with the bottle of tequila around her waist, tugged her against his side, and led her straight to the front door.

And *out* the front door.

CHAPTER TEN

Kaydon

"I—"

She cut herself off again after that single letter, and he made a mental note, a promise that he was going to find a way to support her finishing those sentences, those protests and questions and whatever thoughts were bouncing around in that magnificently complicated brain of hers.

But before he could do that, he needed to get her *out* of her brain.

"This way," he said when she faltered on the front porch.

"I'll go home," she murmured. "You don't have to throw me out."

That stopped him dead.

That had him dropping his arm and turning to face her in shock. "What part of the last week has told you that I want to throw you out?"

"The part where you dragged me through the front door?" she muttered.

"Or," he said, wrapping his arm around her, "is it because I'm taking you somewhere special and the fastest way to get there is through this gate?" He released her, opened the wooden panel with a flourish, and nudged her beyond it.

"I—" Her mouth opened and closed.

"Tell me, sweetcheeks," he ordered, albeit gently.

She stared up at him, lips parted, glasses slipping down her nose.

He pushed them up with his pinky, taking care to not whack her in the face with the bottle—that would certainly put a damper on both of their evenings. "Tell me," he said again.

"I don't understand you," she whispered.

There.

That was something. A full sentence, and one that made sense under the circumstances.

"Good," he said, tucking the bottle under his arm and tugging a lock of her hair. "Now, come on." He wove their fingers together, drew her forward into his back yard. This was one of his favorite things about the house, right up there with the hidden library, but also, the space was the reason he'd bought the home in the first place.

The inside could be—and had been—fixed up.

The yard, the old-growth trees, the lush garden with its gazebo covered with vines and intertwined with twinkling fairy lights would be much harder to replicate. It was easy to put in a door, shelves, to buy a chair. Plants, on the other hand, only grew so fast. So, the back yard had been a major perk, not to mention…

He plugged in a code, unlocked another gate, and—

"Wow," she whispered.

That had been his reaction, too.

Kaydon nudged her toward the edge of the hot tub. "Socks and boots off. Feet in. Tequila incoming."

"I…" A breath, her glasses pushed back up her nose, giving him a flash of that little bee on her finger. "This is probably a bad idea."

"Then we'll have bad ideas together."

"What if my phone goes off again?"

"Do you think it was an emergency?" He probably should have asked that earlier.

"No," she whispered. "It was my mom. She's...she gets unhappy if I don't immediately answer, but..." A sigh, quiet and drawn-out. "I don't want to talk to her. There's a reason I moved across the country." He waited. "I needed some distance. They—*she*—can be a lot."

"I get that she's a lot," he said gently, "but she called three times, and once more as I shut your phone away. Is that something you need to check on?"

A shudder. "God, no. She's just upset because I didn't answer."

"Sure?"

She nodded. "I'm sure."

"Okay then." Kaydon smiled and gave her another nudge. "Socks and shoes off. Feet in."

Scar hesitated, her blue eyes on him, those damned glasses sliding down her nose again. He pushed them back up. They gave her sexy librarian vibes and made him have the urge to be naughty in order to be smacked with a ruler over his knuckles...or maybe to swat her ass with one. But they were leaving little red creases on the bridge of her nose, and they might fog from the heat of the hot tub he was trying to coax her into.

Coils of steam rising from the water, the plants growing tightly around the tub, leaving only a few feet between them and the heated space. The tile making up the floor and lining the edges of the hot tub was brightly printed and reminded him of when he'd visited Morocco. Swirls and splashes of color. Cheerful. Maybe even a little loud.

But somehow it fit perfectly in this little oasis.

"Can you see without those?" he asked when she started to toe off her shoes. "Without your glasses?" he added when she glanced up at him.

"Yeah," she murmured. "You might go a little blurry at the edges."

"All the better," he teased. "Then you're not looking at my ugly mug."

She scoffed. "You already know you're the most handsome man I've ever seen. I swear to God people could do their washing on the lines of your jaw, it's so fiercely defined."

He wasn't sure about that. But he couldn't lie and say that her calling him the most handsome man she'd ever seen didn't make him feel good. More than that, though, he could also play along...even if it meant acting like a dumbass while doing it. Kay lifted his shirt, asked innocently, "What about if you did your laundry here?" Yes, he was showing off. No, he didn't care. He worked hard for his body, and since she seemed to like it, he might as well give her a show...

Red on her cheeks.

Her fingers clenching and unclenching at her sides.

Then she glanced up at him and...giggled. And yeah, he'd totally show off and make a fool out of himself and play along and strip off his shirt any chance he got if it made her laugh like that. Because the sound of her giggle was waves crashing into a shoreline, birds chirping in the early morning, the pages of a book turning, the goal song when he scored, the crowd's cheers rumbling through him, hurting his ears, filling him with adrenaline from his head to his toes.

The sound filled *him* up.

No adrenaline. No chasing a high.

Just a sense of utter rightness.

While he was absorbing that, she bent—still smiling—and pulled off her socks. He took off his own shoes and socks, moving to the side of the hot tub and the table that was almost hidden amongst the greenery, dragging it forward and turning to ask—

"Holy shit," he whispered.

Sweats were puddled on the ground. A sweatshirt and tee

next to them, the boots nicely aligned, socks tucked into the openings. Her glasses sat on top of them. And…Scarlett—*Scar* stood there in simple panties and a sports bra. White cotton covering her breasts, patterned fabric of little cartoon dancing sushi rolls covering her bottom. Nothing overtly sexy about either garment, but it was still sexier than any lingerie he'd ever seen a woman wear. Faint outlines of her nipples pressing into the bra where her breasts stretched the material taut, making his mouth water. The soft curve of her belly exposed, along with her narrow waist, and flared hips that screamed for a man to grip as he pounded into her from behind. Freckles dotting her pale skin like they were a roadmap to her heart. A small tattoo on her rib cage, intertwined writing he couldn't decipher from ten feet away…and then didn't get a chance to as she sank down onto the hot tub's edge and slid into the hot water.

The table dropped and nearly tipped over when he forgot he'd been carrying it, the soft splash of her nearly naked body making him lose all sense of reality.

His cock thrummed in time to his heartbeat, a steady pulse that made it nearly impossible for him to steady the glasses, the bottle of tequila, to take a second—and a breath—before bringing it over to the hot tub.

Another breath before he could confidently set the bottle and shot glasses on the tub's edge.

Still more before he could go to the waterproof bin and pull out two towels, which he then set on the table to be close at hand, but not at risk of getting wet.

Then another before he sat down and pulled off his own shoes and socks, plunking his feet into the water and watching Scar.

She sat on the far side, her eyes closed, head tilted back, the ends of her bright red hair dipping into the water growing darker—more auburn than copper. Her throat was slender. Her lips pink and tipping up at the corners. Her breasts, still encased in that material, didn't really float, but the rounded globes peeked out above the surface of the water, glistening skin that screamed out to be touched, to be kissed and licked and stroked.

More blood to his cock.

She was a fucking tease.

Even without trying to be.

"Are you getting in?" she asked softly.

If he got into that hot tub, he'd be getting into her. There was nothing else to it. He'd fuck her until they were both senseless, until the ache in his balls was finally gone, until she was too limp and relaxed to worry about her phone or her brain or how she thought she was a disaster.

But he wasn't sure that fucking her would bring trust.

"Scar," he murmured.

Her hands disappeared beneath the surface of the water and then reappeared, fingers gripping the band of her sports bra. It went up and over her head, landing on the tile next to him with a wet *thunk*. "I don't need the tequila, Kaydon," she said softly. "I just…" A long, slow breath. "I think I just need you."

He was on his feet.

He didn't know how he got there, didn't realize he was moving. One second his feet had been in the hot water. The next he was ripping off his sweats, yanking off his shirt. One more, and he was waist-deep in the tub, water sloshing around his hips as he propelled himself toward Scar and took her in his arms.

"I want this," she whispered. "I want you. But," she added, placing a finger over his mouth when he bent to taste her, to give her him, "please"—her voice dropped even lower— "please, just don't hate me when this is all over."

This wasn't *ever* going to be over.

He was going to make sure of that.

But now wasn't the time for that conversation.

Already, his cock was throbbing, his head spinning, his

nerves on sensory overload having her almost naked body pressed to his almost naked body.

"Kiss me."

Her voice strengthened and rose. Her arms wrapped around his shoulders, pulled him toward her.

And then she kissed him.

CHAPTER ELEVEN

Scar

THIS WAS CRITICALLY STUPID.

This also was the best kiss in the history of all kisses.

Yeah, maybe she would end up in ashes, reduced to rubble and ruins at the end of this, but she'd also have the memory of *this*.

Of Kaydon's arms banding tight. Of his momentary surprise when her lips hit his before he recovered and began kissing her back, his tongue slipping into her mouth, teasing along the side of hers, flicking and coaxing and then—thank *God*—fucking her mouth like his tongue was his cock and she was on the receiving end of all that glorious, hard pounding.

One of his hands went to her hair, the other slid down the side, palming her ass, hitching one of her legs around his waist.

Then the other so she was straddling his hips, so that his cock was pressing against her pussy. Even with both of them still wearing underwear, it was still the best thing ever. Hard and hot, long and pulsing. Hitting her in just the right spot as he slowly thrust against her that she couldn't hold on to the kiss, couldn't have her mouth fucked at the same time he was working her. She broke the kiss, her head dropping back, her legs tightening.

Overhead, the sky was darkening, she noticed through eyes gone blurry.

Partly because she didn't have her glasses. Partly because what Kaydon was doing between her thighs had her ready to explode.

His fingers bit into her scalp, tiny hurts that had goose bumps prickling on her skin, her pussy going even wetter. Her nipples ached, desperate for sensation. And even as she grasped on to that thought, as her brain was still trying to formulate the words to send down to her tongue, Kay shifted, perching on the edge of the seat in the water, taking her into his lap, and dragging his mouth along her throat, her collarbones, the vee between her breasts.

He nuzzled at her flesh, the damp heat of his mouth competing with that of the tub, prickling over her skin, causing her hips to buck against him.

And then he tilted his head and sucked one of her nipples into his mouth.

Sensation exploded.

Lights flashed behind her eyes.

Her legs tightened, and she couldn't stop herself from finding a rhythm, from riding his cock as he lavished her breast. Her orgasm was already close, so damned close, and whether it was from the margaritas earlier, the sexual tension of the last year, the kiss at the rink, the closeness in his library, or her finally saying fuck all to every bit of prevarication and just finally fucking going for it, she didn't know.

It was there.

It was close.

She *needed* to come.

His palm dropped to her hip, not stopping her motions, but encouraging them. "That's right, sweetcheeks," he said, releasing her. "Do you feel how hard I am for you? Do you feel how much I want you?" He sucked her nipple deep, fingers massaging her breast, drifting over to tease her other one. Between the roughened tips, the callouses flooding her nerve endings with pleasure, the liquid heat of his mouth, and the hot water sloshing around her, she was overloaded.

With desire.

With need.

With *pleasure.*

"Kaydon," she moaned, rocking against him.

"Keep going, baby," he ordered. "Keep going."

She *couldn't* stop. Even if an asteroid was barreling toward them, their deaths imminent, she couldn't stop, couldn't prevent herself from plummeting over the precipice and falling into a cloud of bliss.

Scar cried out, her fingers digging into his arms, his mouth still working on her nipple, tongue and teeth drawing out the pleasure, extending the moment as wave after wave of her orgasm hit her. It seemed to go on forever as she rocked against him, as she rode the hard length of his cock until finally, she collapsed against him, limp and satiated and…

"Did I die?" she whispered.

He chuckled as he smoothed a hand down her hair, straightened away from her breasts, and tugged her close, resting his chin on top of her head. "No. But I will if I don't get to see you come again."

One movement had her up against his chest.

Another had her in his arms, and he climbed out of the tub and strode through the greenery surrounding the space, along a narrow path she hadn't noticed.

The cool evening air bit at her skin, threatened to pull her out of bliss and back into spiraling, but luckily the walk was almost nonexistent. One moment he was on the path, and the next he was yanking open a door, flicking on a light, and…

"Oh," she breathed as he set her down on a smooth wooden bench.

Dry heat surrounded her, immediately making her mouth feel parched. A gust of cool air alleviated it for a moment, but only for a moment because then Kaydon returned to the sauna with two towels, and the door clicked closed behind him, the heat settling again.

He spooned some water on the rocks in the corner, sizzling filling the air, and instead of oppressive heat, the space became pleasantly warm and damp. Trickles of water and sweat slid down her body, slid down *his* body, his abs, and she found herself on her feet, moving toward him, running a hand down his front.

His boxer briefs were plastered to his body, outlining his erection and making her mouth water.

He'd gotten to taste.

She hadn't.

She needed to get her fair share in, to feed the monster inside her that was desperate for this man with every *single* cell in her body, to taste and feel and hold and touch because that wouldn't always be available to her.

So, she needed to be greedy *now*.

Needed to have her turn before it was too late.

"Scar," he murmured, hand sliding up her spine, drifting into her hair again, the other slipping down, dipping into her underwear.

"No," she whispered, shimmying to dislodge his hold.

"Okay, sweetcheeks," he said. "No rush. No need to go furth—*ah!*"

She'd dropped to her knees, yanked down his boxers, and sucked his cock deep into her mouth. He was thick and hard and tasted like salt and man and something she knew would be forever engrained on her taste buds, something that was intrinsically Kaydon. Gripping him tightly, she jacked him as she dragged her mouth up and down his length, sucking hard, taking him as deeply as she could, until she had to fight back the urge to gag, until her lashes went damp with tears. Deeper than she had ever done before, but his sounds of pleasure, the soft groans, the way his hand had come to the back of her head, resting but not pushing her down, even though his fingers kept lightly clenching and then opening in time to his moans, had her pushing *herself*.

Deeper.

Faster.

Harder.

His hips jerked, and she couldn't hold back the cough, the gag, and then his hands were on her shoulders. "Shit," he rasped, "I'm so—"

She brushed him away, gripped his cock again, and went back to what she'd been doing, adding her tongue, flicking her wrist, taking him deep and ignoring the tears that dripped down her cheeks.

"Scar, baby," he panted. "You don't have—"

She slid back slowly, sucking as hard as she could, reaching in to lightly cup his balls.

"Oh fuck," he gasped.

Even deeper this time, breathing through her nose making it easier, or maybe it was easier because he liked it so much, because she liked bringing him pleasure, loved making him lose himself, was fucking addicted to discovering what he liked and what had him faltering on the edge of control, his hips bucking, his hands clenching, curses tumbling out of his mouth.

"Scar," he warned, and she noted the edge of warning in his voice, the way he was trembling, his fingers gripping her hair tightly, his eyes locked onto her as she blew him, every muscle in his body taut and standing out in sharp relief.

It was the sexiest fucking thing she'd seen in her life.

But she wanted to watch him lose that final bit of control.

So, she dragged her tongue along his shaft, jerking and sucking him deeply as quickly as she could, clenching him tight, massaging his balls, slipping a finger back to lightly press on the spot behind them.

He jerked, pressed himself deeper into her throat.

But he didn't pull away, didn't tell her to stop, and the groans and curses tumbling through the air told her that he liked it.

So, she kept going.

And *going*. Ignoring that her mascara had certainly run, that she probably had drool on her chin, that his underwear was tangled around his ankles and hers was still on.

This wasn't pretty or controlled or perfect.

This wasn't some requisite return of pleasure.

This was giving Kay a piece of her, making him feel good, and feeling like a fucking queen because she could make him lose control, give him that pleasure, just as he'd given it to her.

Relaxing her throat, she released her grip, brought her free hand to his hip, and tugged him lightly forward, knowing that he'd understand, knowing that he'd start fucking her mouth. And he didn't miss a beat, just joined in on the rhythm she'd started, thrusting between her lips, hitting the back of her throat as she sucked him down, brought him even deeper.

And deeper.

And deeper.

And—

"Fuck. *Scar!*"

He exploded. Cum filled her mouth, and she swallowed him, the saltiness of him clinging to her tongue, slipping down her throat even hotter than the air of the sauna, the water of the tub.

Curses were pouring out of his mouth, his hands still in her hair, his hips still gently thrusting.

Then she was tugged off him, yanked into his arms, his lips on hers, his tongue sweeping and yanking her into a kiss that had her seeing stars.

"Scar," he murmured when they broke for air, gently tugging her against his chest. "My fucking Scar."

And then he released her, wrapped her in a towel, and set her on the bench.

And…she fell.

Headfirst.

Heart first.

CHAPTER TWELVE

Kaydon

"TOMORROW, OKAY?" he murmured, shifting closer and nuzzling her throat.

Because she smelled like vanilla and his cologne and *Scar,* and he didn't want to forget the special blend…and hell, truthfully, he was just looking for another excuse to touch her, to get his lips on her skin.

They'd sat in the sauna until they were both lightheaded—him mostly because she'd given him an orgasm that sucked several years of life out of him. Her most likely from the heat itself.

When they'd stumbled into the cool air, shivering with just a towel wrapped around their bodies, his mind had cleared.

His need hadn't, though.

He wanted her more than ever.

But…slow. Building trust.

So, he'd scooped her up into his arms, carried her through the back yard (going the long way because he didn't want to give the neighbors a show with his beautiful Scar clad only in a towel), and then had thanked God that he'd had a keypad installed for the back door for just this reason.

He'd punched the combination, let them in, and then deposited her in the shower, thanking God a second time that he'd installed the instant hot water system because it had immediately stopped her teeth from chattering.

One long shower later—also thanking the heavenly spirit for having that tankless water heater—they'd stumbled into the bedroom.

His cock had been hard and aching.

She'd been lax and half-asleep.

So, he'd dried her off, slipped her into a pair of his sweats and some socks, and tugged a T-shirt and hoodie over her head.

She should have looked ridiculous in clothes that were three sizes too big, but instead, she was adorable—a precious object he wanted to lock up in his house—in his library, perhaps—and keep her safe forever.

He'd wanted to keep her at his place, to go grab that tequila and maybe DoorDash in some food and curl up on the couch.

But they'd skipped a dozen steps, and so when she had yawned and burrowed into him while he dried her hair, he'd known he should take her home.

Now they were on her porch, and he was trying to pry himself away.

"I...um...do you"—she yawned again—"want to come in?"

He did. More than anything. And maybe a better man would refuse, would kiss her outside her front door and then go home. He may not be the best, may not be one of those men who always did the right thing every single time, but he could read this woman.

And he knew that despite the yawn, it had taken her a boatload of courage to ask him to come in.

"Yeah, sweetcheeks," he said, "I really could use a cup of coffee."

A flicker in her eyes—relief, fear, gratitude, insecurity? Probably all of those, given all that she had shared earlier. "Okay," she whispered, pushing open the door and gesturing him inside.

He noticed she had a little bench by her door and smiled, knowing that its presence would make his mother happy. *"Where are people supposed to sit down to take off their shoes, Kaydon?"* she'd asked when visiting his new house for the first time. Then, mysteriously, one had appeared by his front door when he'd returned home from practice.

Funny how that worked.

But Scar already had one, and he knew that would please his mom.

Funny how that *also* worked, how he wanted Scar to fit in with his family, to fold her into his life so that she didn't want to leave, to give her something it appeared she didn't have with her own parents.

Anyone having that thought this soon after starting things with a woman should be worried, or at least have his head examined.

It was too fast. Too much. Too soon.

But, fuck it. When a man knew, he knew.

And he knew that Scar was it.

Was that terrifying? Yes. But only because he was terrified that he wasn't going to proceed carefully enough and would fuck things up. It had taken a year for him to get her to admit that she didn't hate him, that she was avoiding him not because she didn't like him, but because she *did* like him. And he still hadn't gotten her to actually agree to a date.

He'd finagled his way into dinner, into more time.

"Kitchen's this way," she murmured, brushing by him and walking down the hall.

There looked to be a dozen DIY projects that were halfway completed. The living room was half-painted—two walls covered in a soft gray, the other two patched and primed over what must have been an intense red. The thermostat was hanging off the wall, wires exposed, a new smart one sitting on the floor beneath it and covered with sheetrock dust. Several pictures were stacked along the hallway; a hammer and a plastic box of small brass nails and 3M strips sat nearby. Plastic covered a doorway farther down with a stack of tile sitting just outside the frame. He turned into her kitchen and saw that it extended to that room as well. The backsplash was half-finished, packets of new knobs were scattered around, and several of the doors appeared freshly painted and were sitting on top of a drop cloth-covered island.

Scar glanced around and winced, tiredness fading as embarrassment took its place. She pushed up her glasses. "Sorry," she whispered. "I forgot that this was..." She trailed off. "Such a mess," she eventually finished, her gaze sliding to the side.

"Where are your coffee mugs?"

Her brows drew down. "What?"

"Coffee, sweetcheeks," he reminded her.

"I—um—" Her eyes slid closed and then back open. "Right. Coffee." She spun around and opened a cabinet, pulling down a little basket with an assortment of Keurig pods. "Pick your poison," she said, turning again, this time to flip up a piece of plastic that had been covering the coffee maker. After that was revealed, she turned to another cupboard and pulled out two mugs.

One had the Gold Hockey logo.

The other was emblazoned with, *This Bitch is a Unicorn*, and had a picture of a sassy-looking redhead wearing a unicorn horn, sparkly rainbows shooting from her breasts.

Kaydon could vouch for the fact that Scar's breasts should be shooting rainbows.

They were round and perky and filled his palms and had the perfect amount of jiggle and her nipples were...

His cock twitched.

He cleared his throat...and the memories from his mind.

There would be more time with Scar and her rainbow-esque breasts soon.

"Let me guess," he said, clearing his throat again when the words sounded like they were rasped out. "That one was a gift from Rebecca."

She glanced down at the mug and then more pink drifted onto her cheeks. "Um, no, actually. I bought them myself." A shrug. "I sort of have a thing for mugs."

He filed that piece of information away as he moved toward her, trapping her between the counter and his body and scanning the contents of the cupboard she'd pulled the mugs out of. There were a plethora of quippy cups.

I have neither the time nor the crayons to explain this to you.
Taco dirty to me.
I don't have a dirty mind, I have a sexy imagination.

Toward the back of the shelf, there was even one with a cartoon of Santa and fancy script writing surrounding the image that said, *None for you, bitch.*

He laughed out loud at that one, tugging it down and swapping it for the Gold mug. "I think this one is my favorite."

"It's not even near Christmas," she murmured, hips canting back.

And *that* wasn't helping his cock twitching.

He shifted away, waited until she'd turned to snag the two mugs and bring them to the coffee pot. "My mom would say that August is the beginning of the holiday season," he said. "And since we're nearly in September, that's a full month of Christmas prep that I've missed."

A ghost of a smile as she followed him, picking up the basket of pods. "Your mom sounds awesome."

He snagged the basket from her, held it up so she could choose before selecting his own variety. "She *is* awesome," he said. "Especially considering the six of us turned out to be decent human beings."

"I don't know about that," Scar teased, and he relaxed

slightly, happy that the more time they spent together, the easier it seemed for her to be able to move beyond the awkwardness she so obviously felt. More time. More patience. More margaritas and orgasms and coffee mugs. Yeah, he could do that. "But," she went on, "I suppose that you're all right." A beat. "At least, for a hockey player."

Gasping, he snagged her pod from her and plunked it into the Keurig, pushing down the handle and starting the coffee brewing. "How dare you?" he grumbled, sliding her unicorn mug in. "Hockey players are the toughest athletes around. We stand in front of hundred-mile-per-hour slap shots for God's sake. Willingly."

"Tell that to the baseball players. They stand in front of one-hundred-and-*twenty*-mile-per-hour baseballs flying at them, with *no* padding—"

"Some of them wear that elbow thing," he grumbled as her coffee percolated.

"And you have a full set of gear," she pointed out.

"We also strap blades to our feet," he pointed out to *her* pointing out.

"That's true," she said, swapping out her mug and putting in his pod, along with his cup onto the stand. "But then that just means that you whine about the edges not being right like ninety percent of the time."

"Whine—" He broke off and let out a growl. "How *dare* you!"

She'd been about to take a sip of her brew, but he snatched it —carefully, so as not to burn her—away from her, set the mug on the counter, and then scooped her up, tossing her over his shoulder.

Scar squealed, and he swatted her lightly on her behind, then tickled her waist as he carried her into the living room. "Whine?" he growled again. "*Whine?*" He tossed her gently on the couch then came down on top of her. "Whine?" he repeated more gently as he realized what he was doing, how it might make her shut down, to retreat.

She didn't.

The little beast nipped his nose, her eyes sparkling, her lips curving before she said, "Yes. *Whining*."

And then she kissed him.

CHAPTER THIRTEEN

Scar

"Are you sure you know what you're doing?" she asked.

Not because the work that he was doing wasn't gorgeous—she sure as hell hadn't gotten the tile she'd installed on her backsplash to look so even (which was most of the reason it was sitting there, half-finished, her anxiety about the shoddy job making it nearly impossible for her to finish it, to finish *anything,* lest at the end of it, she disappointed herself with the work, like she'd disappointed everyone else in her life).

Happy thoughts, that.

Enough, she reminded herself, forcing her brain to get right off that shit show of a train of thinking.

But, rather, she asked because he was covered in Spackle.

Absolutely *covered* in it.

All over his arms, on his jaw, in his hair, on the tip of his nose, streaked across his T-shirt, his sweats. He looked like he'd gotten more on himself than the wall.

Though the *wall* looked fabulous.

The glass subway tiles were perfectly aligned in the offset pattern she'd tried to do herself but had only ended up looking like a jumbled mess. He'd popped those off, managing to save more than she had hoped. Not that she hadn't had extras because she'd bought for the very possibility that she would fuck up the project (no surprise there). Now he was just putting in a few pieces around the outlets, while she finished painting the cabinet doors that had been sitting on her island for a good month.

Because she'd wanted to do it herself.

Because she *could* do it herself.

Maybe she wasn't the best tile setter, but she could paint like a champ. It was just…she'd…what?

Admit it, Andrews, her brain commanded.

She hadn't wanted her disappointments in her face. Because it wasn't just that she was worried about disappointing herself, like her parents, like those failed relationships. It was about seeing those disappointments in her life every *single* day. The glaring reminders.

Which was why she'd been so reticent with Kaydon.

At least with her other failed relationships, she could cut ties, could let them go and not worry about their worlds intertwining.

But with Kaydon…for nine months out of the year, they saw each other almost every day.

Maybe it was just in passing, maybe it was for a press event, mostly it was him on the ice while she was doing something in the rink. But he was there, near her, woven into her job description, and she had to at least minimally (since that's what she'd been doing for the last season) interact with him. She loved her job. She really liked him. Hell, if she were being truthful, in her non-spiraling-for-once brain, she *loved* a lot of things about him.

His smile.

His gorgeous face and body.

Everything she'd seen so far that was beneath the beautiful window dressing. His heart, the way he helped with Fanny's classes, how he talked to the kids and never missed a charity event for the team. How he worked his ass off on the ice, never failed to sign autographs or stay after to talk to a fan, how he'd overcome his injury and became a better player for it—generous, smart, beyond skilled. He was an asset to the team, and not just because he could put pucks into the net.

He was the heart.

She'd been around long enough to understand that different players had roles on the team. Some—like Max Montgomery—were comic relief. Others—like Brit Plantain (the BAMF, the only female in the league) were the spine. Unwavering strength whether the team was winning or losing. Some ground out their play, were the structure and supporting beams of the team's foundation—Logan and Ethan. Others were the muscles and nerves—quick jolts of energy and skill, scoring and speed. Coop, Liam, and Kevin came to mind.

And then there was Kaydon.

Who'd battled. Who'd seen more downs than ups. Who'd fought for his place and was the better for it.

He was the heart.

Kaydon was what pumped lifeblood through the team, helping it through to its next stage as the lifers, Stefan and Blane, and—after this next season—Max, retired.

Kaydon was about the furthest thing from a disappointment as she'd ever come across.

So, when he'd shown interest in her?

Yeah. Cue panic.

But now...yes, she still had panic, but it was a controlled sort of descent into her mind, a careful slip into the mud pit of fear at her center, her nails trying to find purchase along the edges, even as her body weight dragged her down. She was going to get dirty. She was going to slosh around in that pit like it was some special sort of medicinal mud that would make her skin smooth and glossy and radiant.

Then she was going to jump into the hot tub, the sauna, the shower.

Wash away that fear and sludge and only be left with radiance.

She was going to do that because she liked Kaydon, because they worked together, and she loved her job.

But—and she was starting to finally come to terms with the fact that this was the most important piece for her spiraling mind to understand—she was going to come out of this liking —*loving*—one thing about herself.

Just one.

Because she needed to find that about herself, needed to *truly* believe it.

Otherwise, the spiraling, the *cycling* would win.

And she didn't want to spend the rest of her life feeling like shit, like a disappointment, like a disaster, even if those descriptions were apt.

One thing.

That was all she had to find.

And if, at the end, she was still covered in that mud, if it turned out to be slop that pigs preferred rather than fancy medicinal shit, she would wash it off and hope like hell that she at least got a bit of radiance for her trouble.

———

"I'M GOING TO GO," Kaydon murmured.

Probably because she'd just yawned for the fiftieth time in that last ten minutes. It was after midnight. She'd painted cabinets. He'd installed backsplash. They'd both screwed in knobs.

And with the exception of the tile needing grout, her kitchen was back together.

No plastic on the counters. No tarp on the island.

No boxes of tiles or knobs or hinges scattered around.

Everything was put away, dusted off, and...she wasn't disappointed.

So *not* disappointed that when Kay suggested they order in

some food and then finish painting her living room while streaming action movies in the background, she'd agreed.

A week ago, she'd fretted over the color and had halted painting, wanting to sit on it before finishing the other walls.

Today, her storm cloud gray covered the walls.

And it went perfectly with her pale blue couch, her graphite throw pillows, her gray and blue patterned area rug (pulled forward slightly to cover the splooge of paint she'd dropped onto the wood floor and couldn't quite get all the way off).

A blemish hidden beneath something pretty.

Why did that feel like an apt description?

But it was another room done, and another disappointment stifled, especially when Kaydon said he knew of something to remove paint from floors and had some at his house after he'd touched up his walls and done some splooging of his own (also, why did that sound like it should be on a porn stream site?).

So pretty soon, the blemish would be gone.

And she really hoped *that* would be an apt description. Sooner rather than later, hopefully.

Tonight, however, she'd probably come as far as she was able. She was covered in as much paint as Kaydon was covered in Spackle, and she should probably feel guilty about getting two of his sets of clothes dirty (since she was still wearing his lovely smelling clothing), but the fact was that she wasn't giving them back.

He'd put them on her body.

They now belonged to her.

So there.

Plus, her clothes were sitting in a pile in his laundry room, after he'd gone to retrieve her glasses and both sets of their clothes after their shower, so he was doing some clothes hostage taking of his own.

Now, with *Die Hard* something playing in the background (she'd lost count sometime during the painting), the sound of bullets and explosions were drowning out the pounding of her heart.

Because she didn't want him to go.

Because he'd promised tomorrow earlier, but really, there was no guarantee that he'd wake up in the morning and still want to see her again—especially when she'd basically used him as free labor for her house for the entire evening.

Fingers brushing along her jaw, drifting back to weave their way into her hair, pressing lightly on her scalp as he tilted her head back and searched her gaze. "Or," he murmured, "I could stay."

"I—" She broke off, throat spasming.

He didn't look away, didn't speak, but she saw something like anger in his eyes, and then her words came fast and furious and so rapidly they were practically jumbled all together.

"I'm tired. You're tired. You should get home before you're *too* tired and can't safely drive, and I'm sure your knee is hurting you. Mandy would probably kill me if she knew that I'd willingly let you up on a ladder a month before the season started. Especially, when you've finally been feeling a hundred percent and your rehab is complete." She sucked in a breath and kept going. "And I'm sure you're sweaty and want to take a shower and change into fresh clothes. And you probably want to relax in your own house. And—"

"I'm not going," he said.

She kept talking. "I shouldn't have kept you here this lo—*ah!*"

He scooped her up again, only this time they didn't end up on the couch.

This time they walked down the hall—well, *he* walked. She was carried, bobbing along with every step and he strode toward…

Her bedroom.

CHAPTER FOURTEEN

Kaydon

HE *SHOULD GO.*

He should quit while he was ahead.

But...he couldn't look at the disappointment on Scarlett's face and not do something to make it better.

He needed to sweep that hurt away. He *needed* to wrap her in bubble wrap so no one and nothing could ever hurt her again. He needed—

To make sure he didn't whack her head against the door-frame, as he turned sideways and slid into her bedroom. He'd walked by the space earlier that evening, taking an inspection of the other projects she had half-completed.

This room was the only one without drop cloths and plastic sheets, that had four walls that were all painted—a pale turquoise that looked killer with the soft yellow and pale pink accents (not something that he would have ever thought looked good together, but also something that went amazingly well with one another, especially when adding in the brass lamps and old-fashioned brass bed frame). The comforter was some sort of floral mix, and it was loaded with pillows that picked up on all the colors, even the brass of the bed.

But he wasn't interested in the bed.

Or—at least—not *only* the bed.

First, he had to take care of the paint covering her body. Which meant that he had to get this woman in the shower. Oh, the humanity, he had to see her naked and wet for a third time in the day (though one of those times was only half-naked, so really, he was only getting to see her naked two and a half times, and that meant he was due another half-time at some point in the future).

Still carrying her, he moved through the door into what he presumed was the bathroom—mostly presuming because he could see the outline of a sink through the opening, flicked on the light, and…stopped.

Dead in his tracks.

What the actual fuck?

There was a hopscotch pattern of tiles leading across the floor to a shower…that wasn't a shower. Oh, the showerhead was there, along with the handle to turn on the water. But there wasn't any floor in the shower, nor was there a curtain or glass walls. Just the showerhead and studs.

Next to which sat a bathtub that was fully finished, complete with candles and fresh flowers sitting in a vase on the surround, a paperback open and slung over the edge, a fluffy rug in front of it.

He spun, barely reacting in time to not whack her head on the doorframe, and studied the sink he'd only seen a shadow of before and saw that the vanity too was completely finished—a marble top, a mirror hung above it, a turquoise toothbrush holder and soap dispenser, and one of those glass things that held Q-tips all stacked neatly on the top.

"Does the toilet work?" he asked.

A long pause. "The one down the hall does."

He closed his eyes, stifled the shake of his head. "Right," he murmured, making a mental note to his To-Do list for the following day. Bathroom floor. Toilet. *Shower* floor. Get someone to come over and put glass in.

Then he strode forward and set her on the rug. "I'm guessing the tub works?" he asked as he straightened, steadying her with his hands on her hips.

She swallowed and nodded. "Yes. With hot water and everything."

Kaydon didn't ask if that meant she'd spent an extended period of time *without* hot water. Instead, he just had her sit on the edge of the tub and turned on the taps, testing the water as it took an unearthly amount of time going from cold to hot.

Eventually, however, it did, and he fussed with the knobs until the water was the correct temperature.

"Right," he murmured, gripping the hem of her (well, *his*, but really, he'd already marked it over to her in his mind) sweatshirt and tugged it up and over her head. Next, were her shoes and socks. Then her sweats, her shirt.

She wasn't wearing underwear—a fact he'd forgotten until just that moment, something that would have made working on her backsplash and painting those walls a lot harder to concentrate on if he'd remembered earlier. Luckily, he hadn't. Because now her kitchen was together and since he also had what appeared to be a never-ending list of things to finish (not that she would ask, not that he cared if she asked because he was going to do them anyway), starting with the toilet and floor and shower in this bathroom, it was better that he hadn't been distracted by her lack of a bra.

Because Scar had the best tits he'd ever seen.

He'd dreamed of what they looked like, imagined tasting and touching them when he saw them pressing against a sweatshirt, straining against a tee. He loved legs and ass, but, fuck, he loved breasts. Big or small, perky or not. He just wanted to get his mouth and fingers on them, and he sure as shit wouldn't turn down sticking his dick between them and getting his titty fuck on.

Such dangerous thoughts when he was trying to be a gentleman.

Reaching over her, he turned off the taps, checked the water one more time, and then—his voice like fucking gravel—said, "Get in, sweetcheeks."

She studied him for a long moment.

Then brushed her fingers along *his* cheek and smiled. "I think you'd better get in with me."

———

IT WAS MUCH LATER AS he was driving home, clean and still hard because even though she had reached for him, had offered to stroke and suck and kiss him again, she'd also been tired, dark smudges beneath her eyes, her lids heavy and half-mast.

Especially when he'd used every trick in his repertoire to "wash" her skin.

He'd just had to make sure that he got all the dirty spots clean.

And if one of those happened to require him slipping his fingers between her thighs and finger fucking her into an orgasm, then *c'est la vie.*

He'd damn sure made certain that her pussy was clean, too.

Now he had a boner the size of a—insert something large that didn't make him sound like a total bragging douche canoe — roll of quarters? (Snort). A baby's arm? (Gross). A really hard dick that was desperate to be inside that pussy he'd so thoroughly cleaned? (Yeah, that).

But she'd smiled when he'd dried her off.

Smiled again when he tucked her in bed and kissed her forehead.

Smiled a third time when he promised to be back in the morning with Molly's.

Winning her over with tacos and baked goods. That he had absolutely no problem doing. Especially since he had a little more time before he went full-on Nutritionist Rebecca's meal plan and got to reap the benefits alongside her.

Not that he would stop getting them for her after training camp and preseason games and the full swing of the regular season got underway. He would just have to put on his control pants and exercise them to their absolute Spandex potential.

Good thing his ass looked awesome in Spandex.

Now *he* was smiling as he drove the couple of miles to his place, slid through the gate, and made his way to his house.

He'd never look at the hot tub the same—and he sure as fuck wouldn't be able to be in the sauna and not think of Scar's molten mouth sucking him down, her fingers gripping him tight as she jerked him into oblivion.

But it was the library that he stopped by when he walked into his house, the library that he stepped inside.

He strode over to the shelf, to the book she'd left slightly out of place, and picked it up.

The title and cover both seemed innocuous, just one word and a simple flower on the front draped in a ribbon. Maybe it was about a wedding? It looked close enough to be a boutonniere, except for the pearl in the middle of the flower.

Hmm.

Shrugging, he tucked it under his arm, straightened the rest of the books so they were in order, then flicked off the light and left the room.

Upstairs to his bedroom.

He stripped down, brushed his teeth, did his business, and then climbed into bed naked and thinking about everything that had happened with Scar that day.

Thinking how damned lucky he was.

Thinking that he wasn't going to fuck this up.

Thinking…that he'd better get started reading.

CHAPTER FIFTEEN

Scar

SHE WAS ready for the knock on the door.

If she were being truthful, she'd been waiting for it since she'd first woken up an hour before. Waiting since she'd gotten the text:

Good morning, beautiful.

Now she was full Kaydon Coma (or maybe, that should be Kaydon *Koma*) and beyond ready to see the man.

She'd gone from desperate to keep him at a distance to desperate to soak up every single minute with him, no matter how long it lasted, because there would be an expiration date, a shelf life, an end point.

Because she was Scarlett Andrews.

And that was how things worked in her life.

It didn't matter if she was smart (for the record, she was). It didn't matter if she was kind, busted her ass at her job, tried to feed the karmic gods (also, for the record, she did). It didn't even matter what was in her heart and mind and soul (her life was her life and that, unfortunately, was just what it was).

But for now, Kaydon was on her porch and—

"Oh, you wonderful man," she gasped, reaching forward, and grabbing him by the shirt, lifting up on tiptoe and plastering all of her soft, occasionally exercised body over all of his hard,   often-worked-out-and-so-he-was-hard-and-cut-and-glorious torso.

G.L.O.R.I.O.U.S.

She inhaled his scent—fucking *glorious*—and kissed his cheek.

Then she swiped the Molly's bag and swept back into her house, past the fully painted living room, and into the completed (minus the grout in the backsplash) kitchen.

Two plates out of the cupboard and onto the counter.

Two mugs—his had a T-Rex on it with *If you're happy and you know it clap your...aw*, hers was a unicorn with its middle finger up that read *Shuh. Duh. Fuh. Cup.*

One Molly's bag open and the top of an apple cinnamon (with streusel!) muffin into her mouth.

"Should I be lucky that I got you pressing against me and a kiss before you took off with the bag?" Kaydon asked, humor in every syllable, as he took the mugs from her, read the sides, and smiled, then brought them to the coffee maker.

"Yes," she said, downing more muffin.

God, Molly's was the best.

He snagged the basket of pods, pulled out two—one, she noted being the flavor she'd selected from the day before, one, she also noted, being the flavor *he'd* selected the previous evening. She shouldn't be surprised he noticed, that he'd paid attention.

Despite thinking that she hated him—something she supposed would have been easy to assume considering that she had done her level best to avoid him for an entire year—he was very in tune with her. Even while spiraling or struggling to know what to say or freaking the absolute fuck out, he'd been beyond patient.

He was also patient when he got you off, her inner hornball thought. *VERY patient.*

She shivered, because yes, he'd been patient. One even might say *gloriously* patient. And hell, if she kept thinking of the man as glorious or gloriously *something,* she was going to have to wash her brain out with bleach…or at least invest in stock in Thesaurus.com so that she could get some adjectives. And she damned sure better keep all those adjectives in her brain because otherwise, the man was going to get a big head.

Though him having a big head wasn't the worst thing in the world, not when he was thrusting into her mouth how she hoped he'd thrust into her vagina.

Hard. Fierce. Right on the border of too much.

Scar swallowed hard, the muffin turning to dust as another shiver slid through her.

What were carbs (even cinnamon apple carbs) when it compared to the glorious power of Kaydon Lewis?

And seriously, though, she was going to ban herself from saying that word.

At least for the next five minutes.

A kiss to her nape had her trembling. "Cold?" he murmured against her skin.

She shook her head. Not cold in the least. Hell, she felt like she was burning up, and normally, that would have been a pun that had her cackling, but with Kaydon's body behind hers, the coffee brewing, a muffin in her hand, and far too many clothes on their respective frames, she didn't feel like laughing.

"I want you," she whispered. "Why do I want you so much?" She spun so that their fronts were pressed together, their bodies perfectly aligned. "I've never wanted a man as much as I want you, never wanted someone who made me feel this unbalanced and vulnerable and *needy.* I should run, keep on running like I have for the last year"—he sucked in a breath, and she went on—"but I don't *want* to run. Instead, I want to launch myself into your arms and soak up every single inch of you. I want to use you up until you throw me away, and then I want to repeat the process over and over and *over* again."

His eyes were gentle. "Sweetcheeks."

"I know that makes me sound like some creepy stalker who doesn't know the word *no.*" She shoved a hand through her hair. "But I can't find it in me to care enough to back off."

Her chest heaved.

Her hand, skating through her hair, falling back to her side, shook.

Her voice petered out.

Silence fell.

And then he murmured, "Good."

Her mouth dropped open, but only for a moment, because then his fingers were pressing it closed, were skating across her jaw, and dipping behind her ear, into her hair.

"Good," he said again, "because I'm fucking addicted to you, Scar Andrews. I can't stop thinking about *you.* I want *more* until I get you so bound to me that you can't let me go, and then I want to throw on a few more stitches, just for good measure. I want you to not want to let me go because I can't imagine not having you right here, in my arms, your sexy fucking body against mine, your beautiful fucking brain spinning until you're so full of thoughts of *me* that you don't know which way is up." He tugged lightly at her hair. "I want you Superglued into my life, laminated to the plans of my future, concreted into my hot tub—" He broke off. "Okay, that last one sounds exceptionally creepy." A grin that had her breathing slowing, her pulse settling. "I'm not lying when I say I like you, Scar, that I don't care if you think your brain is a mess or that your life is a disaster. I'm here because *I like you.* I'm here because I want to be."

"I—" She started to fumble for words, to lose her train of thought. But then she cleared her throat, swallowed hard, and, for once, just let them come, without trying to make them sound perfect or to meet someone else's expectations.

In that moment, she was just Scar Andrews.

And, somehow, with Kaydon close, his eyes soft and warm and on hers, his body near, that was okay.

"I want you here."

"Good," he said, his fingers flexing. "That changes, you let me know, and I'll back off. Not"—another flex—"because you start running scared or are worried that you're not what I want. But because this isn't working for you, because you're not feeling me the way I'm feeling you. That would suck, sweetcheeks, I'm not gonna lie. And I won't lie and say I wouldn't do my damndest to try and convince you that I *am* what you want." His smile was a punch to the solar plexus, or maybe, warm, rough fingers trailing up her thigh. "But," he said, face going serious. "I also don't want you to be trapped into something you don't want. You want out because you're done, then I'll be out. You try to run scared"—his eyes flared— "and I'm fucking chasing you down, baby because I am going to make you mine."

Make you mine.

Fuck, she wanted that so badly.

"You hear me, sweetcheeks?"

She nodded.

"You get me?"

Another nod.

"Perfect. Then let's stop rehashing this shit. You accept I want to be here, and I'll accept you'll tell me if you don't want me in your space," he murmured, releasing her hair and nuzzling her throat before stepping over to the Keurig and switching pods and mugs. "And then," he said, bringing her mug back over to her (because he'd known which mug she'd intended to be hers), "we get on with just enjoying the shit out of each other."

CHAPTER SIXTEEN

Kaydon

A WEEK LATER, Scar had a shower.

And floor. And a toilet that worked.

She didn't have a guest bathroom that functioned (aside from the toilet), nor a laundry room with a subfloor that was repaired and reinforced enough, the dry rot removed, to actually hold a washer and dryer. But she had the bathroom and the smart thermostat installed and the pictures put up on the wall in her hallway.

He'd been a regular handyman.

His dad would be impressed. He always joked that none of his kids had picked up the handy gene and that they always preferred to just pay someone to do the work.

That normally was the case for Kaydon as well.

It was just…seeing the way Scar had looked at him when he'd finished with that small strip of tile, and he'd felt like he'd hung the fucking moon. *She'd* made him feel that way, and that, along with not wanting her to live in a place where she had to go to one bathroom to use a toilet, and then another to get clean in the mornings and brush her teeth at night (well, in the morning, too, he knew), had made him crazy.

He needed to take care of her.

He could lay some tile, could install a thermostat, and paint, and hang pictures, and set a toilet on a wax ring so that it was functional.

What he *couldn't* do was repair dry rot or install garage doors (or fix his own, for that matter—though, luckily, he'd arranged for someone to look at both doors at both houses the following week). So, the dry rot was in process. The garage door a little further along that process.

And now, he was concentrating on getting that first date.

Or rather, he'd secured it and would be picking her up in half an hour.

They'd spent every night together, eaten and watched movies, painted, and got covered in all sorts of home improvement dust. They'd downed tacos and margaritas and a half-dozen bowls of chips.

But they hadn't sat across a table from each other in nice clothes and talked…about the weather.

God, he hoped they didn't talk about the weather.

Though, he supposed that even talking about the weather with Scar would be interesting. *Everything* about her was interesting. The way she tilted her head slightly when she talked to him. How she frowned when texting into her phone, no matter who was on the receiving end of her messages. Her collection of mugs and her explanation for the bee tattoo (her job had her flitting around like a bee, preparing to sting if someone took on the team). The way she still refused to give him the title of her favorite book—not that he was minding reading through that shelf of novels she'd complimented (so long as he pretended they hadn't first belonged to his mother). How excited she'd been when he'd brought her homemade brownies, and the stomachache they'd both gotten later that night from eating way too many of them.

Her favorite topping on pizza was olives, the weirdo. And she ate the crust first, which wasn't the worst thing he'd ever done, he realized when he tried it upon her insistence. It left the gooey, cheesy middle for last, and he had to admit that he dug it.

He shrugged into his white button-down and fastened it shut, then pulled on his jacket, made sure his beard was in order, his hair under control. He'd made a special trip to his barber up in the city that afternoon, just to make sure he looked nice for her.

Stupid considering she'd seen him sweaty after a game, and that he'd spent the majority of his time in her presence in sweats, a hoodie, and T-shirts. Probably also stupid considering that she'd seen him covered with Spackle and grout and sweat and dust, and apparently still found him attractive. Or at least still kissed him and held him close and writhed against his perpetual erection when they were making out, dust and grime or not.

For the record, her bath was an excellent place to get clean.

Also, for that same record, her hands were as talented as his were at making him "clean."

Knowing he was grinning like a fool and not giving a damn, he shoved his wallet into his back pocket and strode into his kitchen, grabbing his keys off the hook and then into the hall, where he stopped to put on and tie his shoes.

That done, he glanced at his watch, realized he still had twenty minutes before he had to meet her.

And that the three-mile drive would take him, at most, seven minutes.

He knew women, knew that he shouldn't be early and mess up her getting ready schedule. But the thought of waiting another twenty minutes to see her was untenable, so he decided to take his chances and hustled out his front door.

Kay would take the long way, would make sure that he was driving at *exactly* the speed limit.

But it would be bearable because he would know that it was bringing him closer to Scar.

He snorted as he buckled in and started up his car. And *she* was worried about scaring him off? If she knew how often he wanted to handcuff her to him, not to mention how thought out his plan to keep her captive in his library was (he'd mentally created a plan to keep her fed and calculated out how to rig up a bathtub for her, since she was such a fan and had made *him* a big fan of soaking with her for long periods of time)...if she knew those plans, she would be running for the hills.

Should be running.

Definitely addicted. Definitely hooked and reeled in and not giving a fuck.

He pulled out of his driveway.

Took the long way around.

Never once went over the speed limit.

And he still arrived at her house sixteen minutes early.

Okay, so maybe he *had* sped. Just a little. But it wasn't his fault. It was pure Scar and her addictive brain and body and—

"What the fuck?" he breathed as he turned into her driveway and spotted...

Absolute chaos.

CHAPTER SEVENTEEN

Scarlett

HER MOTHER WAS SCREAMING.

Loudly.

And for long enough that Scarlett could hardly discern one word from the next. Or maybe that was because she'd been through this before, had heard it all before.

Knew that there was no way to stop it.

Just…wait it out.

Her makeup was half done—literally half done. As in, only one eye had makeup on it. Her face was covered in primer but no foundation or blush or contour. Her brows were complete at least, and the dark circles beneath her eyes that were the norm were concealed.

No lipstick or mascara.

She was wrapped in a robe, the lingerie she'd picked out to wear beneath the dress that she hoped would have Kaydon's eyes popping out of his skull catching on the silk every time she shifted.

Scarlett tightened the tie and tried to imagine herself as a wall of impenetrable glass, the verbal bullets ricocheting off without hitting her, but try as she might, she couldn't stop herself from hearing them.

"If your brother was alive, *he* would do this," her mother spat, pacing Scarlett's living room while periodically pausing to sniff around the space in disdain.

They'd already established that she didn't like Scarlett's choice of paint color and that her couch was uncomfortable—not that her dad seemed to mind it, seeing as he had parked his ass onto it and pulled out his phone from the moment her mother had started ranting. He wouldn't step in—he never did—he had a fucking advanced degree in avoidance.

At least until it was his turn to pile on.

"Charlie *is* alive," Scarlett began. "He's just working in Korea for six months and—"

"I don't mean *him*," her mother screamed. "*He's* just as much of a disappointment as you are."

"Because he's bi?" she asked softly. *That* had been a whole new layer of disappointing—at least, according to her parents. Scar didn't give a damn who Charlie loved, so long as he *was* loved and found his little slice of happy.

"Because he's weak and impossible." A finger jabbed into her chest as her mother screeched, getting in Scarlett's face. "Just like you."

"Because he wouldn't give you money either?"

Her mother sneered. "*He* would do this!" she yelled. "Heath would *do this!*" Her fingers dug into Scarlett's arms.

Scarlett winced and shifted back, trying to extricate herself, but her mother clung tight.

"I'm not selling my house, Mom. I'm not moving back home," she said, going for calm, but firm, and knowing it wouldn't fucking matter. Because she could scream back, she could cry and be hysterical, and her mother would just continue on with her ranting until she got what she wanted. Scarlett sighed. "I'm done with this. I'm done with you guys doing this to me."

Seeing as she hadn't immediately given in to her mom's histrionics, *now* was the time that her dad would avoid his avoidance and try to play good cop, try to pretend like he gave two shits about her when really, he thought the world revolved around him just as much as her mom did. He was just slier about it—pretended that he wasn't selfish and wouldn't try to drain her dry, but he'd become a fucking vacuum in a second if he thought that it might manipulate her back into his life.

Into his life in a way that got him what he wanted, of course.

Because if she *didn't* give, she was the disappointment, the failure, the child who shouldn't have lived.

"Pumpkin," her father said. "Be reasonable about this. We need the money—"

He kept talking, but she didn't hear him.

Because *be reasonable?* Right.

What they meant was give up everything she had busted her ass for, to give up the distance, the protective barrier she'd erected.

A barrier that was bullshit, given that they'd shown up on her porch without a word—that phone call a week ago (that she'd ignored) the only contact she'd had in close to three years.

Since Heath had died.

Since she'd only given them half of the life insurance money he'd left to her specifically, using the other half to move here, to buy this ramshackle house, to get a fresh start free of the chaos she seemed to wreak no matter her best intentions. She knew Charlie had done the same with his insurance money—half into his savings, half to their parents. So they should be more than settled, have more than enough funds to live their lives.

But it *hadn't* been enough.

They'd cut her off.

She'd licked her wounds, sworn off relationships and friendships and men. She'd had Charlie and that was enough.

Until the Gold had pulled her into their web.

First through casual acquaintance (because PR Rebecca had

seen her work and knew that Scarlett was a pro at putting a veneer on the shittiest of circumstances—hell she could teach a Master Class in it). Then through reluctant friendship—first Rebecca then Fanny then so many of the others. Then...Kaydon.

But she wouldn't be thinking this now if not for the team, the organization, and everyone within it.

The *be reasonable* guilt trip probably would have worked if she hadn't been where she was for the last few years. If she hadn't begun to understand true friendship and how family actually treated each other, hadn't begun to experience it herself.

Because now she understood it was Brit bringing Mandy a coffee and pastry—making a special trip even though she couldn't eat it because she was on the meal plan—just because Mandy was exhausted, and Brit knew she needed a little special treatment. It was Coop hiring a night nurse to give Calle a break and then sending her on a girl's weekend. It was Rebecca making brownies on the guys' Cheat Day so they could all partake. It was Liam being Mia's karate dummy, to be pinned and thrown around and pretending to play the bad guy for her students, even though he was tired from a long road trip and just wanted to rest. It was Char inviting Scarlett to the team events and everyone making her feel like she belonged (even if deep down the niggle of feeling like an outsider or interloper or a ticking time bomb of disappointment destined to go off at any given time never quite went away). It was Brandon sitting in the rink for hours on end, working there instead of his plush office because it brought him closer to Fanny.

Family was chipping in when things got hard. It was giving more than taking—though it was also knowing when it was their turn to take...and being sure to not take too much.

It was tears for a teammate suffering a loss.

It was cheering on a support staff's kid for being the first person in their family to graduate from college.

It was donating equipment and time and energy and cheer

to people who needed it because that made the world a better place.

It was Kaydon fixing her backsplash and stealing kisses while painting walls. It was him looking at her with patience and kindness and bringing her muffins and remembering that she liked to use her unicorn mugs.

It was...her—her finding the strength to push beyond her past, to put aside how she'd grown up, to find the courage to hope. Because, God, she didn't want to keep doing *this*, having this scene, being manipulated and yelled at and feeling like shit all the time. She didn't feel like shit when she was with Kaydon or Fanny or Coop or Mandy or Brit or...any of them.

Only with these two people in front of her.

She had to find the strength to hope that this wouldn't end in disappointment (even if she was prepared for it).

Find hope that she could pull her shit together—and keep it locked up tight.

Find the hope that this scene in front of her could just be...done.

Done.

D.O.N.E.

The light bulb clicked on in her brain.

It *could* be done. This *could* be the last time she allowed this to control her. It could be the final moment she let her parents give her a swirly in the fucked-up toilet that had been her childhood.

She...could be done.

Why? As in, why had she never realized that before? Why hadn't she understood that just because they were toxic, didn't mean that she had to continually bring those toxic people into her life. She was part of the Gold, had been enfolded into their family, and she hadn't made the situation with them go bad, turn toxic. This was less about her and more about what she was willing to put up with. What she was willing to *give*. Because it was only herself that was holding back those final pieces, not allowing herself to be vulnerable, to be all in.

Because she'd known that she would disappoint them.

Well, fuck that.

She wasn't toxic.

Maybe she'd chosen to be around toxic people, had allowed herself to be swept into that fucked-up web of bullshit her parents seemed to thrive in.

But she wasn't going to allow that any longer.

It was...done.

"I want you to leave," she said, interrupting her dad in the middle of his diatribe. He had continued talking and cajoling and convincing and trying to wear her down the entire time she'd been coming to a realization in her mind, the entire time she'd been spiraling—for once in a good way. He hadn't recognized she wasn't with him.

Hadn't cared, probably.

Because even as she interrupted him, even as she repeated that she wanted them to leave, more surety in her tone, he huffed out a sigh, sauntered back over to the couch, and pulled his phone out again.

Avoidance 2.0.

Only instead of avoiding her screeching mother, he was avoiding what Scar had said.

She'd given in, folded, crumpled so many fucking times.

So why would they expect that this time she'd finally worked out one small piece of the fucked-up puzzle of her mind?

They wouldn't, of course.

Now, she just had to make them.

First step of that was getting them the fuck out of her house before her date because she wanted it to be fabulous and to *look* fabulous. She wanted Kaydon to be hard all night thinking of her. She wanted him to imagine what she had on underneath her dress.

She *didn't* want him to show up with her makeup half-done, her hair in disarray, and her shitty parents there.

"Mom, Dad," she said, cutting her mother's wailing about how they weren't going to be able to put food on their table and did Scarlett *want* her parents to starve. Meanwhile, Scar had seen the pictures on Facebook, knew they'd just returned from a two-week cruise. She wasn't doing this again. When Heath had gotten sick, he'd urged her to move. She'd stayed because he was her brother and he had always been the one awesome thing in her life.

But when he'd died...there hadn't been any reason to stay.

And even in his death, he'd tried to take care of her. He *had*. He'd given her the means to leave.

"You need to get out of my house," she said, and for once, she didn't have to steady her voice, stamp out a quiver in her tone. Done. She was *so* fucking done. "If you don't go"—she increased the volume as her mom tried to shout over her—"I'm calling the police, and I will have them escort you off my property."

"Your *property*," her mother spat, "was bought with *my* money. Mine. This should have been *mine*. I puked for months with him. *I* got the stretch marks and saggy boobs. I get the wrecked vag—"

"I believe that Scar asked you to leave."

Neutral, almost spoken softly, but there was something powerful about his voice—about *Kaydon's* voice that stopped the room cold.

She whirled, winced when his eyes searched her face, knowing exactly what he saw: half-done, half-formed, half-complete, half...woman.

He stepped forward, pressed a kiss to her forehead. "Go get ready, sweetcheeks," he said. "I've got this."

"But my parents—"

"I heard enough to deduce that, Scar baby—"

"Her *name* is Scarlett. If you're going to fuck my daughter, then you might as well use the name *I* picked out for her. It's the least you can do to show respect for me—"

Kaydon snorted, and God, she could love the man for it. "Respect is earned," he said and turned his back on Scar's mother. "Sweetcheeks," he repeated, "go finish getting ready."

"I—"

"Trust me?"

Deep chocolate eyes full of hope and affection and…respect.

She'd earned his respect.

She could trust him, at least a little bit (*A lot!* her mind shouted). She'd earned his respect. He'd earned her trust.

Scar could work with that.

Turning on her heel, she left the room, went upstairs, and finished getting ready.

And all the while, her heart was in the living room.

CHAPTER EIGHTEEN

Kaydon

HE STARED AT THE WOMAN, who gave him a glimpse of what Scar would look like in forty years.

Still beautiful—the delicate cheekbones and tipped up nose and freckles gorgeous, even marred with a few wrinkles.

What made her ugly, though, was her expression.

One Scar would never wear. He was certain of that down to the marrow of his bones.

Now this woman—who could be a fucking supermodel—stared down over that delicate, tipped-up nose of hers at him in disdain and shot arrows at him with her eyes.

"*You* need to leave," she ordered. "This is between our daughter and ourselves"—she waved a hand at the lump on the couch, and Kaydon might have felt a little bad for the fucker if not for the fact that he'd just heard the asshole trying to sweet-talk his way into getting Scar to sell her house. The house that because of *these* people she hadn't been able to finish, she was so crippled by whatever fucked-up thoughts they'd surgically implanted into her mind. And no, he didn't know that for sure (aside from the fact that it was certainly less surgical implanting and more emotional abuse) since she hadn't shared everything that had gone down in her life up to that point—only that she had been seen as a disappointment and a disaster and felt like she never measured up. But he'd seen enough, watched her fight through those emotions and the darkness weighing her down enough to understand that *these people* were the cause of it.

The evidence was right in front of him.

It was in the way they'd spoken to her, the fuckery of tag-teaming like they knew that if they could just berate and push and cajole and break her down enough that she would give in.

She would blame herself and do something she didn't want to do.

Because *they'd* made her see herself that way.

Because *they* were the worst sort of people.

But then—and he was so fucking proud of her for this—he'd been about to step in, to demand they back the fuck up and get the fuck out of her house when Scar had lifted her chin. She'd straightened her shoulders. She'd balled her fingers of one hand in the hem of her shirt and used her others to push up her glasses.

And she'd ordered them out of her house.

Calmly. But definitely an order, all the necessary strength imbued into her tone.

He'd gotten to step in then. To play the hero—at least a little bit. Because she'd been the hero first. Because she'd laid the groundwork, taken that first step, leaped off the cliff.

He just got to be her parachute.

He pulled out his phone, hit a number he had on speed dial.

"What are you doing?" Scar's mom sputtered—and hell, he hadn't even gotten her name and he was kicking her out of Scar's house.

There was some sort of poetic justice in that.

"I'm calling the police," he told her.

"Hello?" came the voice in his ear.

"What?" Scar's dad asked, straightening and finally tearing his attention off his phone screen.

"Scott," he said, "it's Kaydon."

"Hi, bud," his friend—and a police officer (though, based on the time, Kaydon assumed he was technically currently off-duty) said. "What's up?"

"Look, I'm at my girlfriend's house (more assumptions, but if Scar thought that at the end of this she wouldn't be his girlfriend, then the woman was…going to be his anyway)," he said. "Her parents are here unannounced. They don't get along, and Scar has asked them to leave several times. *I've* asked them to leave" —he held her mother's gaze—"but they're refusing. Normally, I'd call this in, but since you live just around the corner from my place, and her house is at 6572 Vineyard, and we're going to be late for our dinner reservations, I was hoping…"

There was the sound of locks bleeping, a door opening and closing. "I'll be there in five. Plus is I just got off a double, so I'm still in uniform and have a squad car."

"Room for both of them in the back?"

Scott laughed. "If need be."

"Thanks, man. Tickets for you, yeah?"

Another laugh. "Good ones, yeah?"

"On it."

He hung up, kept his phone in his hand, just in case they tried to do anything crazy, and then went and waited by the front door.

Scar's parents had convened by the couch and were whispering to each other rapidly.

Kaydon didn't give a shit what they were saying. He just wanted them gone so that he could see to Scar, make sure she was good.

Fuck, so much revealed in what he'd overheard.

A brother who'd died.

Charlie gone for six months. He sort of remembered Fanny

mentioning that since they were close, but that was when he'd thought that Scar hated him, so he hadn't really filed that away to study at a later date.

But she was alone with these fucking scavengers who'd hurt her and wanted her to—

He sucked in a breath, released it slowly, and kept half an eye on Scar's parents and the rest of his focus on the driveway. They were getting ready to do something, he was sure of it. Silently, he turned on the camera on his phone and started recording. A black guy in a white woman's house, with two fucking schemers like her parents, especially when he was an athlete and had money they probably wanted?

Well, he wasn't going to be a dumbass.

He was going to *cover* his ass.

After what seemed like an eternity, but was really just a few minutes, he heard a car pulling up, saw Scott climb out and amble up to the driveway.

"Nice place," Scott murmured, shaking Kay's hand.

"It is," Kaydon agreed.

A flick of Scott's eyes over his shoulder. "That them?"

"Yeah."

"And where's your girlfriend?" he asked.

"I sent her upstairs to finish getting read—"

"I'm here."

Kaydon turned…and oh holy fuck. His vision blacked out. His dick decided it was time to rise up and salute the goddess in front of him. His hands ached to touch, and even as he took a step toward her to do just that, Scott whistled softly, snapping Kay out of his fog.

"Fuck, sweetcheeks," he muttered, leaning close and kissing her lightly, "you'll kill a man in that dress."

Scar blushed, whispered, and he was relieved in a way that hit his heart but totally didn't help his cock, "Wait until you see what's underneath it."

His fingers tightened; he nipped her bottom lip. "Just for that, I'm going to make you wait even longer for my cock."

Her eyes went wide. "Kay," she began, and he knew she was feeling it as much as him.

They'd kissed. He'd licked her. She'd sucked him. He touched every inch of her—just to be certain she was clean in the shower...just to be certain he got to feel her pussy convulsing around his fingers.

But they hadn't had sex.

Because...trust.

He knew he'd had it when she'd agreed to it the night before.

He'd had that feeling confirmed when she went upstairs and left him with her parents.

He knew it with that dress and the smart comment.

So yeah, he was desperate to fuck her, but he didn't mind drawing out the anticipation. Especially when he'd get to unwrap her at the end of the night.

"No, sweetcheeks," he whispered into her ear, lightly coasting his hand down her spine, drawing her closer to his body, letting her feel exactly what that dress did to him, "I think we need to take a little more time."

"I—"

Scott cleared his thought.

Kaydon *thunked* back into his body, remembered the situation, her ass-wipe parents, and realized his phone was still recording video. Quickly, he shut it off, deleting the recording, stowing it in his pocket. He had two witnesses now. He didn't need the backup.

Slipping an arm around Scar's waist, he turned her so that she was sandwiched between himself and Scott. "This is Scar," he said, introducing them. "Scar, baby, this is Scott."

"Hi, Scott."

"Can you tell me what's going on?" Scott asked in a far gentler tone than Kaydon had ever heard the man use.

"Those are my parents," she said, sighing. "They showed up and are upset that I won't sell my house and give them money." She sounded tired, and God, he wanted to tuck her into his chest and tell her that he would take care of this whole mess for her, that she didn't need to put herself through this. "I've asked them to leave. Kaydon has asked them to leave. They've refused—"

"I did *not* refuse," Scar's mom snapped, coming over, her husband at her shoulder. "And this is *our* house—"

"Is your name on the deed?" Scott asked.

Scar's mom waved a hand. "No."

"Then what makes you think this is your house? Do you have a rental agreement? Pay the mortgage? The property taxes? The electrical, gas, or water?"

Fuck, Scott was good.

Especially when Scar's mom could only sputter in response and shake her head.

"Then I suggest you listen to the woman whose name *is* on the mortgage." He cut a glance toward Scar. "I'm assuming you pay all of those."

Scar nodded. "Every last one."

Scott turned back to her parents. "Then, folks, I don't see any reason for you both to be here."

Silence in response.

Then Scar's mother opened her mouth, as though readying herself to say something. Before she could, however, Scar's dad dropped a hand onto her shoulder and said, "We'll just get going then."

Scott nodded. "That seems like a good idea."

Scar's mother shot them all a look that should have filleted them where they stood, but she didn't protest when her husband guided her out the front door, across the porch, and out onto the street to their sedan.

"Want me to send a car by later?" Scott asked, "just to make sure everything is all right?"

Scar shook her head. "No." A sigh. "They do this. Push me and then disappear for a length of time. I'm sure I won't see them for a while."

Kay could tell that Scott didn't like that admission, and for that matter, neither did he. How long was *a while*? How often did they show up and berate her like that? How often did they refuse to leave? Or…had Scar just always given in?

Tonight's show of strength seemed to have genuinely perplexed those assholes of human beings.

"Three years," she said as they started up the car and drove away, answering the question that had been in Kaydon's mind —and probably Scott, given the dark look on his friend's face. "It had been three years since the last time."

Scott shifted, reaching into his pocket and retrieving a business card. He extended it to Scar. "In case Kaydon's not around to call me, my cell is on the back. Any time, day or night, okay?"

"Okay," she whispered. "I…" A breath. "Thank you for coming."

Scott nodded, glanced at Kaydon. "Take care of her, okay?"

"On it."

"And on the glass, got it?"

Kaydon grinned. "Got it."

Scott waved and slipped out the front door, striding over to the police car and hopping into the front seat. With a nod, he turned on the engine and drove away, leaving Kaydon and Scarlett all dressed up and ready for their first date.

At least until Scar slipped out of his hold and crossed her arms. "I can take care of myself, you know."

He bit back a grin. "I know."

"I don't need the *men*"—she did air quotes—"to step in and fight my battles for me. I was handling them and—"

"I *know*, sweetcheeks."

God, she killed him with that flush, with the way it appeared on her cheeks regardless of the emotion—or rather, for any plethora of emotions. Anger. Embarrassment. Arousal. Hell, she got flushed when he made her laugh.

He loved it.

Loved to trace the pink swathes on her skin.

With his fingers. With his tongue.

"Then why did you swoop in and rescue me from my parents?"

He stepped toward her, cupped one of those sweet cheeks in his palm. "Because I'm really hungry, and I don't want to miss our reservation." Her mouth dropped open, and he gave into his grin, letting her know he was teasing, but he didn't stop with the lightness. Because after the scene with her folks, she needed to be pulled out of it, needed to have humor weave its way back in. He smoothed his fingers over her hair, brushed a kiss to that tipped-up nose. "Plus, it was totally worth fending off your mother and probably making the worst first impression ever"—not that he cared—"in order to get you in that dress. To *see* you in that dress. To imagine stripping it off you—"

"I thought you were going to make me *wait* for your cock," she said, rolling her eyes, though her breathing hitched when he pressed a kiss to the base of her jaw.

"Yeah," he said. "I am." A beat. A nip to that delicate skin. "I'm just not going to make you wait very long."

She snorted, but that sound cut off when he sucked lightly, when he flicked his tongue out to taste her.

"Let's go," he said, "before we really miss our reservation."

Scar nodded, and a moment later, she was bundled in her coat, the front door was shut and locked, and they were walking to his car.

"Sweetcheeks?"

She stopped, glanced up at him.

"I only played backup," he murmured. "You're the one who swooped in and rescued yourself."

CHAPTER NINETEEN

Scar

THEY'D MADE it to dinner.

She was dressed—all the way (she even had makeup on *both* her eyes, go her!).

But though the restaurant was gorgeous, the food five-star, she couldn't taste a damned thing. She couldn't see the expensive chandeliers, not when Kaydon was in front of her. Couldn't hear the soft music twinkling through the space on hidden speakers, not when she kept hearing Kaydon's words.

You're the one who swooped in and rescued yourself.

She hadn't.

Had she?

She—

Warm fingers on hers. "What do you want for dessert?" he asked.

She'd spent the meal being drawn into conversation with him, the charming fucker, even though her mind continued to circle back to, *you're the one who swooped in and rescued yourself,* to the way he'd stood firm for her, had spoken quietly, but firmly. That continued to battle with the way he'd looked when he'd seen her in the dress, the words he'd whispered for her ears only.

He should be running after that scene.

He was…unfazed.

How? *How?*

"I want you," she said, sliding her foot up his ankle, her leg firmly hidden beneath the long tablecloth. Up again, drifting along his calf, his knee, his thigh.

Kaydon grinned and captured her wayward ankle, ringing it with his fingers and tugging her slightly forward so that it rested in his lap. She slid her chair in, jostling her foot, and she shivered, feeling the hard jut of his erection pressed against her skin.

His slacks hid nothing.

"I'm the *dessert* dessert," he said roughly. "What about anything off the actual dessert *menu?*"

Everything she'd eaten that night had tasted like cardboard —throwing some chocolate and ice cream into the mix wasn't going to remedy that.

She shook her head. "Can we go sit in your sauna?"

His fingers spasmed on her leg. "Tease," he accused lightly.

"Only if I plan on not following through." She shifted her foot, running the side of it along the hard length of him, careful to not poke him with her heel. "I plan on following through, Kaydon. Tonight." She pressed into his lap.

He squirmed, eyes going molten. Then reached into his pocket, yanked out his wallet, and tossed some bills on the table. *Too* many bills from what she saw in a quick glance, but she didn't have time for much more than that before he pushed her foot from his lap, set it on the floor, and rounded the table.

A hand in hers, tugging her to her feet.

A warm chest pressed to her back, hot words whispered in her ear, his slack-covered cock pressed to the small of her ass. "Do you feel what you do to me? Feel my cock so hard and aching, desperate for you that I don't even care that the entire restaurant might see me sporting a hard ass dick."

She gasped.

He nipped the back of her ear.

"*You* do this to me, Scar," he said hotly, his words scorching puffs against her nape, her earlobe, her jaw. "*Only* you."

Her knees trembled, and she suddenly felt very unsteady on the high, high heels she was wearing.

But he had her—*of course* he had her—winding an arm around her waist, steadying her even before she could wobble, as he pushed open the door and led them to the valet podium.

The cool air did nothing to cool her desire, even though she wasn't wearing her coat. It was draped over his arm, along with her purse, details that she'd completely forgotten about, but because he was Kaydon, he'd remembered, he'd taken care.

Of her.

With her.

His car was brought to the front of the restaurant and in the next moment they were inside, buckled up, and zooming off to his house.

She was trembling with need.

Absolutely shaking with it.

Was it the week of foreplay? Was it just because she had wanted him desperately for so much longer than that? Was it... some mysterious connection, something only revealed by the first electric kiss a few weeks before, as though the touch of their lips had fused some unbreakable bond between them and they would only be satisfied once they had each other, once they were bound to each other forever?

She hoped for the last.

She knew she read far too many books.

But...it felt partly true. Kaydon was different. She was different with him, and...right now that was enough of a categorization of what was between them.

His hand dropped onto her thigh—her bare thigh since her

skirt had risen up—and she jumped at the contact of that hot, rough palm. Then relaxed, legs slipping open when he gently stroked his fingers in and out of the inside of her leg. Her goose bumps had goose bumps. Her pussy ached, desperate for her to clamp her thighs together and ease the ache.

But that might stop the movement, might halt those gentle strokes that were slowly easing higher, slowly inching the skirt of her dress up.

Closer and closer.

Higher and higher.

She gasped when they brushed the gusset of her panties.

"Christ, you're soaked," he muttered, slipping a finger under the hem, sliding it lightly over her labia. She shivered, and he pulled his hand free.

"No!" she moaned.

But his hand was only off her long enough to turn on the heater, to point the vents at her, and then it was sliding back up her thigh, more quickly this time, that finger returning.

"I wasn't cold," she whispered, hips jerking when he began lightly stroking again. *God*, she liked it when he did that. Loved that he'd discovered the spots that made her go wild, spots *she* hadn't even known she had until Kaydon had worked his magic, until they'd decided to join in on the going wild party.

She imagined them, imagined her erogenous spots, in an arena—a tiny pair of boobs in a sparkly outfit, a miniature vagina with weird legs that made it look like a perverse Mr. Peanut. Both jumping up and down, waving tiny posters as they watched from the nosebleeds, cheering Kaydon on…and every once in a while, one of them got a backstage pass and could join in on the party.

This just in…she was losing it.

This just in…if Kay kept doing what he was doing, she didn't care.

"No?" he murmured, and she struggled for a moment, trying to remember what in the fuck all she'd been saying because he was stroking a finger up through her folds, then in when they immediately parted, revealing the damp heat of her pussy. Cold. *Cold.* He'd thought she was cold and had stopped touching her because of it.

"Not cold." Her head flopped back in the seat when he slowly dragged that finger up, circling her clit.

"Got it," he said, and faintly she saw the lights around them dim as they got off the freeway, started climbing the road to his place. "Not…" He pressed lightly, and she arched, a moan tumbling off her lips. "Cold."

Another press had her arching again, her hips bucking, desperate for purchase, for more contact from his fingers, his thumbs, his palm.

But he was already gliding away, tracing down through her pussy, circling her entrance, then—

"Kaydon!" she cried as he thrust one thick finger inside her.

Immediately, she began convulsing, clamping around the digit, her body moving, thrusting her pussy against him. His thumb slid up, rubbed at her clit, even as he fucked her with first one finger and then another.

Hard and fast.

Without mercy, he dragged her up, hurtled her toward an orgasm. She didn't give a shit that someone might see her, that anyone could just look in the car and watch Kaydon stick his fingers inside her.

She only cared about that release, that need, that…

The car slowed, and she barely registered him taking his hand off the steering wheel in order to open the gate. All she knew was that he didn't stop finger fucking her, didn't falter in the rhythm that was slowly driving her insane as it propelled her right up to an edge that spoke of her complete and utter decimation.

This man was going to destroy her.

And she welcomed that devastation.

Winding up, driving up through a road at nearly the same

pace as she approached that ledge, and then slowing. The car. His fingers.

But not *her* pace. That didn't slow. Her protests filled the interior of the vehicle, desperate pleas that seemed to have no effect on him. He didn't speed up. The car shuddered as he put it in park. Her pussy was jostled as he pulled back his hand—

"No!" she moaned again, and barely had the word crossed her lips than her seat belt was unbuckled, her body yanked sideways, and his mouth—*oh fuck his mouth*—was on her, nudging her underwear to the side in order to lap up her heat. His tongue delved into her, hands gripping her hips, angling her in the tight confines of the car so that he could absolutely devour her pussy.

Long, deep sucks on her clit.

Shifting down to fuck her with his tongue.

Those fingers biting fiercely into her skin, probably tightly enough to leave bruises, but she only urged him on, only was desperate for him to fuck her faster, hold her hard, suck her deeper.

More.

More.

More.

He bit down on her clit, a sharp stab of pain that sent her up, sent her over, sent her straight into oblivion.

Pleasure spun out of control, filling her abdomen, shooting through her limbs, her fingers, and her toes. Her vision went blurry. Her already fuzzy brain went fuzzier as wave after wave of bliss flowed through her. It seemed to go on and on, and she couldn't breathe—or maybe she couldn't catch her breath. But then it slowly began to ebb, to recede back into the depths of her body.

She managed to lift her head, realized that her neck was aching from being twisted in her seat, her body pretzeled over the console.

That ache disappeared when she saw Kaydon had shoved

his own seat back, had balled his body up so that he could position himself between her legs, and the sight of him, his lips glistening, his eyes threatening to scorch her to ash, had moisture gushing into her pussy.

Which Kaydon seemed to realize.

Because he groaned, dipped his head, and laved his tongue up through her labia. "Fuck," he said, "I wish my garage door was fixed."

She blinked, realized they were in the driveway.

A nip to her thigh. "Because," he rasped out. "I would fuck you right here."

More moisture.

More heat.

More need coiling low and deep.

She spread her legs, ignored the gearshift poking into her lower back, and said, "Well, why don't you?"

CHAPTER TWENTY

Kaydon

"WELL, WHY DON'T YOU?"

His cock nearly exploded at the languid statement.

This woman was going to be the death of him.

"Because," he said, straightening and tugging her into his lap, "we're in my front yard, and I don't want to give the neighbors a show with my O face."

He popped the door, shoved it wide.

She wrapped her arms around him, nuzzled his throat. "But *my* O face is acceptable to show off?" she asked archly.

"Yours is pretty." He kissed the top of her head before levering them both out of the car, and it was a minor miracle that he was able to get them both out with neither of them cracking a skull against the frame. "Mine," he said, kicking the door shut with his foot and moving up the walk to the house, "would frighten small children."

"I'm sure that watching us have sex would frighten a lot of people," she said dryly.

"Bullshit." He fumbled with the keypad before getting the

code in and pushing in through the door. "You're the stuff of fantasies."

Her eyes went half-mast. "Kay," she breathed.

He kicked *that* door shut, fumbled again, though this time it was to flip the lock rather than open it, before he strode for the stairs and carried her up them. He made his way down the hall, into his bedroom, and dropped her on the bed. Not bothering to flick on the light, not bothering with their shoes, he lowered himself on top of her.

"You are," he murmured. "I dreamed about you so many times I half expect to wake up and find myself alone, that I made this all up. That—"

She weaved her hands into his hair and kissed him.

Long and slow with lots of tongue and teeth. This wasn't a sweet kiss, wasn't gentle and loving. It was a demand, a plundering, a retribution.

His life would never be the same.

Shoving at his chest, Scar sat up, clamping her hands onto his face, holding him tight so that she could kiss him within an inch of his life. He was a mountain after an avalanche, the landscape forever changed as parts of himself slid down and away at the speed of light, altering him in a way that meant he would never just be Kaydon again.

She did all that with a kiss.

And then she broke away, leaned over to the nightstand, and flicked on the light.

"There," she whispered, "so you know this isn't a dream."

He loved this woman.

Had probably fallen for her the first time he'd seen her push those adorable glasses up on her nose. Had certainly been in deep when he'd seen beneath the veneer.

But this? *This?*

Her looking out for him, no matter in how small a way, and he was gone. Plummeting, buried beneath that sheet of ice.

"I love you."

She froze when he blurted the words, went so still and blank that he was certain she was one second from pushing him back again, from sprinting from the house.

But then she melted.

That ice turned to liquid and flowed away, leaving a gorgeous, smiling redhead in a sinful dress, who smelled of vanilla and tasted of ambrosia. "Kaydon," she murmured, "I don't think I ever had any chance of keeping my distance from you. Every second, every freaking second I was sliding, inching, creeping into love with you." She placed her palm on his chest, could no doubt feel it pounding beneath his ribs. "I think I loved you from the moment you let Dominic rub his snotty nose on your shoulder."

His chuckle surprised him.

His grin didn't.

Neither did the helium filling his veins, making him feel as though he were floating a thousand feet above the atmosphere, watching his body below.

"Yeah?" he asked.

Her mouth curved. "Or maybe it was when you pulled out a tiny packet of tissues, Kitten. You were so dainty and kitten-like when you wiped yourself clean."

He growled. "You didn't just say that."

She giggled, pushed her glasses up, smirked. "So, what if I did?"

Another growl, mostly because it made her giggle, even if it did make him sound like he was trying to become a Furry. She was happy. He didn't care what he had to do. He just did it, and basked in her laughter, her smile, her joy.

But that didn't mean he was going to let her get away with the sass.

Snagging her around the waist, he drew her toward him, nipped her bottom lip. "I'm going to make you pay for that, sweetcheeks."

Nonplussed, she wove her arms around his shoulders, smiled up at him. "God, I hope so."

A nip to that adorable nose, one hand snagging her glasses and tossing them on the nightstand, his other lifting her up and plopping her onto the pillows.

She squeaked.

"Uh-uh," he said. "I told you earlier I was going to make you pay."

"You *told* me earlier that you were going to make me wait for your cock"—she reached down, palmed him through his slacks—"that doesn't seem to be happening now."

He slid a hand beneath her, reached for the zipper of her dress. "I think you misheard me."

"No—" A gasp when he nipped her bottom lip as he drew down the tab. "I—" Another gasp when he laved her collarbone. "Don't think—" A hiss this time as he parted the fabric, tugged it off her shoulders to reveal the scraps of lace beneath.

Or maybe *he* hissed.

Because she sure as shit had been right about what she was wearing underneath her dress somehow being better.

He hadn't thought it was possible.

But...clearly, he'd been proven wrong.

"Scar," he whispered hoarsely, dragging the material down her torso, over her hips. "My Scar."

Her nipples were pebbled against white lace, a stark contrast to the black of her dress. It was lingerie pretending to be innocent, and it was definitely *all* pretend. Because there was not a fucking thing that was innocent about Scar in those scraps.

Destructive? Yes.

Erasing his control? Oh, fuck yes.

But innocent? Hell no.

He finally managed to get her dress off her legs, chucking it somewhere. So long as it wasn't on her body, he didn't give two shits where it landed.

"Kay?"

"Yeah, baby," he managed, sliding his hands up the miles and miles of exposed skin, trying to figure out where he was going to taste her first. Those toes? Her ankle? Her pussy again? Her hips? Her breasts and throat and nipples and mouth and—

Yes.

Just…*yes.*

All of the above.

"I know you're probably making plans," she said, sliding her hand down his front, yanking the hem of his shirt from his pants. "But, I'd really like it—really *really* like it if you got naked before acting on any of them."

He'd moved before he'd processed leaving the bed, finding his feet on the floor, his fingers on the buttons of his shirt. He was pretty sure he lost about a half-dozen of them in his fumbling to get the material off, in his hurry to yank open his belt, to push down his pants while, at the same time, toeing off his shoes.

Scar watched him with wide eyes.

Probably because he looked ridiculous with his arms and legs flying in all directions, but he persisted, and eventually he was naked and staring down at his woman (who loved him, who *fucking* loved him!) and who was wearing lingerie that was sexy as hell, but that he needed off her sexy as hell body.

Now.

"Kay?" she asked as he was considering the best way to go about that.

"Yeah, sweetcheeks?"

"My bra is a front clasp"—a ghost of a smile—"it's like playing Russian Roulette wearing it." A shrug, her shoulders rotating, and sure as fuck, like she was a goddamned magician, the bra popped open. "Oops," she said, that smile wide. "I don't know *how* that happened."

Kaydon didn't either. Bra clasps were Satan's creation, and sometimes as a grown man (as opposed to a fumbling teenager), he'd still found himself struggling to get them open.

But Scar apparently just had to shrug her shoulders, and magic ensued.

Fuck, why was he standing there pondering magic and clasps when he could have his mouth on her breasts?

No fucking clue, but he was going to remedy that shortly.

He reached for her—

"Kay?" she asked, wrapping her hand around his cock and giving it one long, sure stroke.

"Yeah?" And yeah, it was a fucking rasp. There was no way he was going to survive this, no way he wasn't going to blow in her hand.

"I just wanted to let you know that my panties tie at the sides"—another stroke—"you know, just in case you wanted to get inside them any time soon."

And that was the moment Kaydon's control snapped.

CHAPTER TWENTY-ONE

Scar

SHE KNEW she'd done it the moment she said that because his eyes flared, his cock grew somehow larger in her hand, and somehow...somehow...he was *everywhere.*

Her fingers were brushed off his cock.

Her panties were gone, whooshed away like he was a fucking wizard.

His hands were on her calves, her hips, her thighs, ghosting over every inch of her before sliding between her legs and his thumb unerringly finding her clit.

It was still sensitive from her orgasm in the car, but he didn't go gentle, didn't ease her into it.

He latched onto her nipple, palmed her breast roughly, and made her clit his bitch.

Her head dropped back onto the pillows, her legs spread wide, his name was a benediction, an epithet, a curse, a plea. When she finally managed to cobble together enough sense to remember that she had hands, too, that she had a mouth and could use both to touch *him,* she found herself pinned to the mattress, Kaydon tugging her arms up to the headboard and demanding that she, "Stay."

Not a dog.

Not a *fucking* dog.

But if he gave her orders like that, in that gruff voice, his eyes wild, sweat gleaming on his skin, then she would obey.

Every fucking time.

She clung to the metal railing, knowing he liked the way it lifted her breasts high because he told her, rasping out, "Served up for me, baby. Served up like they are on a fucking silver platter." And then he'd buried his face there, his hot, slick tongue working in tandem with his fingers. The stubble on his cheeks driving her crazy, making her skin so sensitive, making her pussy clench and lament that it was empty.

And all the while his thumb kept up its movements.

Circling.

Pressing.

Flicking.

Driving her right up to the edge, over and over again until she felt like a rubber band pulled tight, like she would snap at any moment.

And just before she got there, he stopped. Time and again until she let go of the headboard, clenched his hair tight, and ordered (yes, it was about fucking time that *she* gave the orders), "Fuck me, Kaydon. Fuck me right now."

He stilled, his lips swollen, his molten eyes meeting hers.

For a second, she thought he would make her wait.

But then he slid up her body, kissed her until her lungs threatened to explode, and then reached for the drawer on the nightstand, yanking it open, fumbling with the contents, things crashing to the floor, before he unearthed a box of condoms, tore the top off, and yanked one out.

It was on his cock a millisecond later.

He was between her thighs a heartbeat after that.

He started to push in, paused, and met her eyes. "Scar?"

"Yeah?" she whispered.

"I love you."

"I—"

He thrust home, and she lost the rest of her words, lost everything except the feeling of him inside her, the way his body pressed to hers, how each stroke felt incredible, how every touch felt reverent, how every second she spent with this man *meant* something.

Meant *everything*.

Meant so much that—if she were being truthful—panic threatened to rise up and suck her down, to take her under, to—

"Scar?"

Her eyes locked with his.

"Stop thinking."

She smiled.

His hand came to her cheek, and then she did it. She stopped thinking.

Just went along for the ride, met him thrust for thrust.

She dragged her nails down his back, harder than she probably should, but he didn't seem to mind. Hell, that was a lie. She *knew* he liked it, not just because he groaned, but because when she did it again, he thrust harder, using his hips to pin her to the bed, pistoning into her so quickly, so roughly that she found herself sliding up the bed, her hair brushing against the headboard, her hands lifting to brace herself.

A nip to her lips had her parting them, had his tongue sliding inside and—yeah, *fuck* yeah—having his tongue fuck her mouth while his cock fucked her pussy was just as incredible as she'd imagined.

Even *more* incredible?

Him rolling to his back, taking her with him, his hands sliding to her hips. "Yeah, sweetcheeks. Let me see those tits. God"—he ratcheted up, buried his face in her breasts—"I fucking love these things."

Roughened fingertips on her nipples, a mouth biting and licking and sucking.

She bucked and took him deeper, seated more heavily onto his waist, their pelvises aligning, his hand slipping down between them and circling, pressing, pinching her clit. So sensitive. Almost too much. But also just perfect, especially with him grinding himself inside her, a slow slide that had her head falling back, her spine arching, her hands resting behind her, just above his knees.

It was there…just there, and she propelled herself toward it. Not waiting. Not standing by and allowing it to happen.

Grabbing hold.

Yanking herself over the edge until…

Free fall.

Her eyes slid closed, her skin went numb, her pussy convulsed and sent out waves of release through her, loosening her limbs, removing the connective tissue between her bones, reducing her into a lump of complete and utter bliss.

Kaydon kept her moving through it, until the very last bit of pleasure began fading.

And then she found herself on her back, one of his hands between her shoulder blades, pressing her up, arching her spine, putting her breasts back on full display. He buried his mouth there at the same time as he thrust into her, almost contorting himself to stroke deep and still tongue her nipples, use his teeth on her flesh. "Fuck, I like fucking you," he murmured against her skin, hips still working her, his cock still pounding into her. "These," he growled, squeezing one breast and then the other with a rough hold that sent her eyes rolling back into her head, "*fuck,* I dream about these. You don't know how many times I've dreamed about fucking them, watching my cum drip down your tits."

Heat arrowed through her; her legs tightened around him. She could picture that, *wanted* that. "Why don't you?" she asked, clenching her inner muscles around him, holding him tight even there.

A groan rumbled through the air. The muscles in his throat stood out sharply. "Because your pussy is even better, sweetcheeks." He yanked her leg from around his waist, shoved it up so that it was folded against her shoulder and fucked her harder. Deeper.

"Oh God," she breathed.

"I'm going to wreck this"—he thrust into her—"for other men." A nip to her lips. "These are going to be mine." He rubbed a thumb over her nipple, pinched it just shy of painfully. "These, too."

She shouldn't be this turned on again already, not from him acting like a fucking caveman. But hell if the possessive way he was looking at her, fucking her, holding her didn't have her ready to come again.

Because the words. The touch. The way that he'd grown wild, his eyes dilating, his body a fucking work of art as he moved over her, *in* her...

And yeah. She was close.

Fucking close.

Kaydon was, too.

She saw it in his eyes, in the tension around his mouth, the little lines that formed just before he was about to blow. She felt it in the strokes—deeper, rougher, faster—and in the way he gripped her tightly and loosely, tightly and loosely.

As though he knew it was too tight but was trying to modulate his strength.

And then he forgot and repeated it.

Over and over again.

Powerful. Hard. Strong. Deep.

He was all of those things.

But the thing that sent her over the edge a second time was that tell, that loss of control, knowing that he was with her and *only* her and that he was diving over the cliff right behind her.

"Come, baby," he ordered, sweat dripping down his temple, his skin glistening in the overhead lights. So fucking gorgeous. So gorgeous *fucking* her. So—

He'd shifted his grip, palmed her ass, fingers spanning almost the entire cheek, and altered the angle of her hips. Just slightly. Barely enough movement that she might not have noticed normally.

But she noticed then.

And noticed big.

"Kaydon!" she cried out, head pressing into the mattress, her nails scoring down his spine, her body and pussy shuddering as she came again.

It was longer, fiercer, more intense, and seemed to go on and on until she couldn't keep her legs around him, until his own thrusting faltered, lost its rhythm, became just a rapid *pound-pound-pound* as he came, too.

His groan sparked embers of pleasure through her.

The way he ground against her, shallow strokes that brought their hips together—fast at first and then slowing, steadying, turning into just pressure.

Just pleasure.

Just—

"Sweetest pussy I've ever had the pleasure to be inside."

Just shivers and aftershocks and a man who knew how to fuck her.

He rolled to the side, wrapped his arms around her and tucked her face into his throat, said softly, "Sweetest woman I've ever had the pleasure of loving."

Shivers and aftershocks, a man who knew how to fuck her...

And a man who knew how to love her.

CHAPTER TWENTY-TWO

Kaydon

HE GLANCED up at the box where he knew Scar was sitting—or at least would be shortly.

She'd been a flurry of activity in the hallway, behind the bench, in the arena itself, taking pictures of kids with their creepy-ass miner mascot. This season they were rolling out a new character (since the pick and maniacal look on the former miner mascot had often scared the shit out of little kids—to the point that the most-liked TikTok of the previous season was a little girl turning the corner on the concourse, seeing it, and then upending her entire bucket of popcorn in an effort to get away from the scary mascot).

Kaydon understood her reaction.

He hadn't liked being anywhere near that foam and psycho-eyed monstrosity.

But now popcorn buckets were safe, a new mascot had been voted on by the public and created, and Scar was on a one-woman mission to get all the kids to like Goldie, the nugget.

The problem was that Goldie looked like a sparkly, mobile turd.

"There is no way PR Rebecca approved that," Coop muttered, rolling out his shoulders and his neck, his gaze pointed in the same direction as Kay's. Though Coop was clearly looking at Goldie, who was dancing in front of the team's box, and not searching the depths of that box for a certain glasses-wearing redhead who had spent the last month driving him crazy (in the best way) while simultaneously addicting him to her.

A drug.

She was *his* drug.

And he wasn't worried about overdosing. There would never be an overdose of Scar.

Everything she showed him, he liked. Well, everything except her parents and the way she thought of herself as a disappointment and had been convinced that he wouldn't like the person she was inside because her mom and dad were total fucking dirtbags.

That he couldn't stand.

The rest of it was perfection.

How she squinted at him sleepily in the morning, her hair mussed up, no matter how many or few hours of sleep they'd gotten. How she'd bought a mug for his place that read, "Real Unicorns have curves," and was printed with a picture of a hippo wearing a fake horn. How she'd bought the soap he liked using and put it in her shower without saying a word. One day it had just been there. Along with a tube of his toothpaste.

There was meal plan food for him in her fridge (because it was about that time to get on track—tonight being the final preseason game before the regular matchups began and things began to count).

She'd bought him pumpkin spice coffee creamer because he was a basic bitch and liked all things PSL.

A pot of Mandy's special bruise cream on the nightstand designated as his.

A drawer for some clothes when he stayed over.

Room on the shoe rack by the door.

Little things that told him she was making plenty of room for him in her life.

And he'd done the same for her, made it clear that he was all in, and if sometimes she seemed like she was waiting for the other shoe to fall, for some sort of disaster to befell them, then Kaydon knew he just needed to be patient.

Needed to give her the time to understand that he was different from her parents, from her exes (and man, those were some doozies).

Eventually, she would trust in them.

He knew she could do it.

She trusted Charlie. Had trusted her brother who'd passed away. Trusted Fanny and Brit and a few of the others.

He could earn a spot amongst them.

He just needed to continue being patient.

A puck clattered against the boards, and Kay had to focus, had to rewind the conversation to remember what Coop—who was now looking at him expectantly—had said.

Glittery turds.

Maniacal mascots.

Right.

"PR Rebecca didn't approve it," he said as Kevin slid onto the bench next to him. Kev nodded in agreement (and since he was married to Rebecca and they had a baby together, his agreement was tantamount to the woman herself agreeing). "Neither did Scar," he said, relaying what Scar had shared with him when she'd paused for a moment to greet him in the hallway. "It was a prototype, and they were supposed to go mascot-less tonight, but the new girl who's supposed to spend the season inside the suit didn't get the memo. She was out there and taking pictures with kids"—and adults—"before Scar realized."

He climbed over the boards and hopped onto the ice.

"Now, apparently, #GlitteryGoldGuano is trending, and there's going to be no taking it back."

"Gotta admit that hashtag is catchy."

"If you say so," Kay said. "I mean, I appreciate the allit-eration—"

"Hey now!" Max jumped in. "No big words. Those are for the brainiac over there"—he tilted his head at Ethan, who'd recently completed his second master's degree.

For fun.

That just didn't compute with Kaydon. He'd made it through school, did okay with his grades, but he'd never will-ingly go back.

He much rather have time to binge bad TV and read and... fuck Scar until she couldn't peel open her eyelids. Not to mention, he now had a built-in DIY project with her house. This week it had been installing a washer/dryer. Last week it had been the tile floor in her spare bathroom. The previous week it had been fixing the railing on the deck in her back yard, and the week before that had been installing a new garage door opener.

Because she'd pitched a fit when he'd sent his guys to install a new door for her—a door she'd only accepted and allowed them to hang because it was special ordered (it wasn't, but a man was allowed a few white lies when dealing with a stub-born one like Scar).

Needless to say, her house was shaping up, *though* she did seem to have a never-ending list of projects she wanted to complete to get it in order. Those projects, which he loved, took mental and physical energy he wasn't used to exerting (at least not when on the ice), and add in his favorite project—fucking Scar until she was limp and relaxed and couldn't open her eyes —and Kaydon was definitely falling into his bed (or hers) every night with relish.

And sleeping right on through.

"How's the knee?"

He blinked, stopped thinking about his favorite extracurric-ular, lest he get a boner and get to experience that fun while wearing a cup, and glanced up at Josh. He was a good guy, though they didn't end up talking a lot because the other man played defense.

"It's fine," he answered immediately, as was his way, as had been ingrained in him. Because if he'd answered truthfully—that it was a little tetchy, probably from hauling Scar's washing machine into place—there'd be problems. He might get to play, but a lot less. He might not get to play at all. He might be back in to see Mandy and Fanny and spend the majority of his free time with two women he respected, but two women who weren't Scar.

He liked them, but they didn't give him orgasms.

Or smiles that lit up his heart.

Or pushed up their glasses in a way that always made him want to kiss them.

"My brother is rehabbing from the same injury," Josh said, kneeling next to Kay on the ice and stretching. "What are his chances of coming back?"

Kaydon had forgotten that Josh's brother played, too.

"He got injured waterskiing, right?"

Josh rolled his eyes. "Kind of. Except it was tubing. The dumb ass got hurt *tubing*. Had one too many beers, decided it was a good idea for one of his buddies to take them for a spin on the lake up there"—he tilted his head in the direction of Tahoe—"He's still with the Rush, and those guys are bad fucking influences. They were all drinking, decided to do some tubing on a lake that's fed from snowmelt. One of the idiots took a turn too hard, and Alexi got tangled in the rope and nearly drowned."

"Fuck," Kaydon said, shaking his head.

"Yeah, you're telling me." Josh stood, shook out his arms and legs.

Kaydon continued his stretching, his exercises that Fanny and Mandy had prescribed. He might be pushing his knee off the ice by installing tile floors and washer/dryers, but he was going to do his best to keep his shit level *on* the ice. "I keep hearing about the Rush," he said, "Skilled guys, but total troublemakers."

Josh nodded, started for the door since the Zamboni was about to drive onto the ice, cutting it one more time before puck drop. "Don't know what the fuck Pierre"—the Gold's owner—"was thinking buying them." Josh scowled. "They aren't Gold material. There's no family or collective hard work. It's everyone for themselves, trying to get into the league, and then fucking off, drinking, and boning as many puck bunnies as possible in their spare time." His scowl deepened. "And I'm including my brother in that category. He's fucking talented, but he can't get out of his own way."

"Hate to say it, but I can't imagine being with the Rush is going to help him with that."

Josh scowled. "Considering he's out for an indeterminate amount of time with a torn ACL and MCL, I'd say you're right."

Kaydon sighed. "Sorry man, that sucks."

Josh shrugged. "For him mostly." A beat. "But also for me because I've got my parents breathing down my neck to use my 'connections' to help him get back to playing." He sighed. "Look, I love my brother. But I have my own life, my own career. I already spent a ton of time getting him in with the surgeon that Gabe"—the team doctor—"recommended, but I don't know what else I can do at this point. It's not my knee that's injured."

"Your brother got a good PT?"

A shrug. "No clue."

Kaydon nodded. Staff and supplies were hit and miss sometimes with those AHL teams. "Maybe ask Mandy for some information. She helped me tremendously. And I'm sure Fanny would be glad to put him through his paces once he's ready to be back on the ice."

Josh clapped him on the back as they strode down the hall. "Should have thought of that myself. Thanks…Kitten."

Max had paused next to the glove drying machine, was

swapping out his gloves for a fresh pair from Richie. He glanced over his shoulder and cackled. "Meow."

Kaydon smacked the back of his head. "Hilarious."

"I know I am."

He turned to Josh, "For what it's worth, maybe Pierre knows what he's doing. He did buy the Gold, after all." Pierre Barie—Brit's father-in-law for those keeping track—had purchased the Gold a number of seasons ago. The Gold had been in their own media firestorm, their former captain (not Stefan Barie, but the captain before him) arrested and on trial for rape, pay- to-play schemes in motion all over the place, a dog-eat-dog environment that didn't serve the players' needs.

Awful.

Kind of like the team Kaydon had played on before coming here.

Probably also why it had taken him a long time to believe the fairy tale the team portrayed, to believe in the spirit of family.

Because it should all be a line.

Instead, it was the truth.

So, the Rush being a bunch of fuck boys who liked to drink as much as they liked to get on the ice, who created havoc wherever they went, and seemed to relish in the chaos...maybe it was the perfect project for Pierre.

He'd rehabbed the Gold.

He could do it for the Rush.

Kaydon was about to say that same thing to Joshua when he stepped into the locker room and stopped dead in his tracks.

His locker was full.

Not of people.

But of Hello Kitty shit. Stuffed toys were crowded on the bench, a set of printed towels were folded and stacked on the shelves above. A banner that had the Y crossed off and an N scrawled in its place was draped artistically across the back wall of his locker. Balloons crowded out the rest of the free space in the cabinet, and…

"Fucking hell," he muttered.

What had he been thinking of about family?

Because hanging on the hook where his jersey would normally be was another sweater—bright pink and patterned in tiny white Hello Kitty heads. Now talk about maniacal. His teammates had picked the creepiest version (probably a knock-off variety) of the normally cute feline.

And they'd plastered a jersey with them.

That jersey also had a nameplate with Kitten embroidered on it, sewn onto its back.

And the number beneath *that?*

Because this whole thing had to turn into some weird sex joke apparently…

That number was sixty-nine.

Of course, it was.

CHAPTER TWENTY-THREE

Scar

SHE'D NEVER REALLY WATCHED hockey before.

Right.

She probably shouldn't admit that, not even in her own mind. Especially since her job was to parcel up the team and sell it to the public in order to get them to come and *watch hockey*.

But truthfully, she wasn't much of a sports person.

Oh, she'd learned enough to understand the game and most of its idiosyncrasies, but she wouldn't ever be the type of person to willingly turn on a sporting event on her TV and sit down and watch it.

She knew that was going to change.

Because now she was *invested*.

Kaydon was down there on the ice, and suddenly she wanted to know what was happening every second, what the thought was behind every play. Oh, and she wanted to storm down there and stab those fuckers who dared hit Kay on the boards.

Why did they have to do it so *hard*?

Regardless, Scar was thankful for the distraction from #GlitteryGoldGuano (which was a sigh-worthy moment she couldn't even begin to process since it was already out in the world and being loved by the Twitterverse, and she knew—just *knew!*—that Goldie was here to stay). She would have been worried that she was about to get fired—because fucking *gold* poop—but Rebecca had already called her and told her to just let it go.

"Mistakes have been made" had been her exact words.

Mistakes were forgetting to tag someone on social media.

Mistakes were *not* giant life-sized piles of poop (and an intern not telling their new costume performer that the mascot was being pulled because it looked…well, looked like a poo).

This delegation thing was a bitch.

She finally understood why Rebecca had worked so many hours for so long. The intern had one job—*one* job!

And #GlitteryGoldGuano was history.

So, she might as well distract herself by watching her man on the ice.

Her man.

That made her smile, and then narrow her eyes at someone who'd come flying up the ice, clipping Kaydon at the Gold's blue line. A hand dropped on her shoulder.

"I don't know who you are, but I know you can't be my sister," a male voice said. "She works during these games. She doesn't slum it by actually *watching hockey.*"

"Charlie!" She jumped to her feet and whirled around, launching herself into her brother's arms. "I didn't know that you were back." She hugged him tight. "Wait," she said. "Why are you here? You have six more months in South Korea."

"What's with the gold poop?"

She narrowed her eyes again, only this time at her brother, and his obvious attempt to sidetrack her. "An intern. And you're only my brother if you ignore the poop."

His mouth twitched. "I don't think that's possible."

"*Make* it possible."

He shrugged, smothered a smile.

She sighed. "You're incorrigible, you know that, right?"

"And yet, you love me."

"Sometimes." She poked his chest. "Now tell me," she ordered. "Why are you back?"

Silence, long enough that she thought he might not answer. Then he did, and…it was total bullshit. "I quit." Another shrug. "Turns out that I'm a California boy through and through."

The words were spoken lightly, his body language screaming casual. Except, there was something off about his eyes, about his smile. "What happened, LiLi? Tell me."

"God, not *that* nickname."

"You love it," she said, ignoring him and pressing on. "Tell me."

A sigh. "Don't worry. It wasn't anything all that exciting," he said, flopping into the chair next to the one she'd been sitting in. "The job wasn't…" He sighed. "It wasn't what I wanted."

The job or something else?

"Charlie," she began.

He reached over and patted the seat. "Stop hovering over me and tell me why you were watching an actual game of hockey instead of snapping pictures of the crowd and the guys on the bench and putting your special social media sauce on them."

Well, damn.

He had to just put it out there like that?

"Um?"

Charlie swiveled in his seat, eyed her closely. "Ah shit, you're blushing. What'd you do? Who'd you meet?" He leaned closer, eyes narrowing. "Who do I have to kill?"

"I—"

But a gasp had her gaze being drawn to the ice, and she was on her feet again in an instant.

Kaydon was sprawled on the ice, legs twisted under him, not moving for one second…two seconds…three—

He popped up and was off and skating, joining his teammates in the rush as they carried the puck into their opponent's end.

"Ah."

She barely tore her eyes from the ice, and she certainly didn't sound the least bit casual when she said, "What?"

Charlie's eyes—so much like her own (minus the glasses)—were knowing. "Don't *what* me, missy."

"I—"

"Went and gave in to your giant crush of one sexy Kaydon Lewis."

"I—"

He put his hand up. "Don't try it."

She sighed, her lips pressed together in a pout. "Fine," she admitted begrudgingly. "I gave in to my crush."

"And?"

Her mouth turned up into a smile. "And what?"

He rolled his eyes. "And *how* is it?"

Her smile widened, and she sighed happily. "He's..." Wonderful. Spectacular. More than she could ever hope for. Great in bed. An awesome kisser. A good person through and through who looked out for her and—

"Fuck, Scar."

She blinked, realized she'd been staring at the ice, watching Kaydon skate again. "What?" she asked, turning back to her brother.

"How the hell am I supposed to kill a man like *that?*"

Another blink. Then she processed. "LiLi," she warned.

"Don't cute sister me," he grumbled. "First, Kaydon is *HOT.* That's hot in all caps. *With* italics. So, if he were dating anyone but my awesomesauce sister, I would hate the bitch." He tugged her ponytail. "But because *you're* the bitch who's dating him, then I'm very happy for you."

"Thanks," she said dryly. "You're so kind."

"Second," he went on, ignoring her as he counted the numbers off on his fingers like he didn't have a care in the world and hadn't just quit a job he'd been so excited to leave for, coming back with shadows in his eyes and sadness in his smile. "Kaydon is a freaking giant, and the man has legs like tree trunks, so please tell me how in the fuck all I'm supposed to play my brother card and properly threaten him, hmm?" He tugged her ponytail again, and she swatted him away. "The man is going to squish me like a bug if I even try!"

"You *won't* try," she pointed out.

"Exactly!" he exclaimed. "Which is reason number three and a really uncool thing for you to do to my masculinity, Scar."

She giggled. "I love you."

He softened, squeezed her hand. "I love you, too," he said before his face went serious. Deadly serious. "But...are you sure, honey? I mean...I want you to be happy, you know I do. But after Mom and Dad and those other guys, I know you like it here in San Francisco, love your job. I don't want you to risk that when the drama inevitably—" He cleared his throat, probably because his words had sliced her deep, so much so that she knew she failed in holding back her wince, the burn in her eyes. "Fuck me, I'm an asshole. Scar"—he squeezed her hand again— "Forget what I said. You're beautiful and smart, and I just want you to be happy."

She nodded, even though pain was still slicing through her center, but she managed to keep her smile. "I'm sure," she said. "I...I admit that I chose poorly in the past, but I'm finally understanding that Mom and Dad played into that."

His brows drew down.

"I thought I deserved that. The drama. The baggage. The chaos." She sighed and glanced down at the ice. Kaydon was on the bench, his eyes on the game. Focused on his job. As he should be. As *she* should be. But she'd finally started to come to terms with this shit, with her past, with the thought distortions that had spent so long careening through her mind.

If she continued to allow them to fester, to swirl and spiral and build, then she would never break this cycle.

So, this—explaining *this*—coming to terms with *this*…it was important. Critically so.

"I don't know that Kaydon and I will have a happily ever after, that we'll get married and have babies—furry or human or feathered." She sucked in a breath, released it slowly. "But I do know that I love him, that he's shown me care and stepped in when everyone else in my life—except you and Heath—has stepped out. No, that's not fair," she added. "Not everyone. Not Fanny or Rebecca or Mandy or Brit. Or the guys. They're all here, have been here, even if I didn't trust it."

Charlie's eyes grew suspiciously wet.

"So, I may have felt like a disappointment for a long time, may have wished that I had died instead of Heath. I may have thought that because it wasn't me, because Mom and Dad thought that I wasn't enough, that I *wasn't*…that I would never be enough, never deserve that happiness." She leaned forward, grasped his hands. "And I got so fucking tired of that. Tired of pretending I didn't want things, until I finally wanted something *so* much, wanted *Kaydon* enough to realize that everything cycling through my head was total bullshit."

"Scar," Charlie whispered, leaning over the arms of their chairs and hugging her tight. "I love you. I'm glad you're here, in this place and happy, and Heath would be, too. It was always us, the three of us against them. Without him, I'll admit I felt a little lost, that I retreated." He pulled back. "I'm so sorry for that. If I knew…if I knew that you were feeling that way…" His lids slid closed, hiding his glistening eyes for a moment. "I should have seen it."

"You wouldn't have."

His eyes opened.

"I was good at hiding it." She pasted a smile on her face. "I *am* good at hiding it. Hell, that's my job"—she threw out a hand —"to package all of this up and make it look good. It's not hard with the guys. They're great. But I'm also great at it, especially with my own stuff."

A frown. "I hate that you are."

Her smile drooped. "I know, and I-I am, too."

Silence fell between them, but the arena was far from quiet. The fans cheered. The players yelled and skated and shot. Whistles blew. Music blared through the loudspeakers.

"LiLi," she said softly. He'd turned away, stared out at the ice, but she knew he was seeing about as much of the game as she was…which at that moment was none of it.

"Yeah?"

"I'm done hiding."

He smiled, and it was his normal Charlie smile, the one that always lit up the room, the one that was contagious enough for her to smile back.

"Well, fuck," he mock-grumbled. "I guess that means I need to hit the gym so that I can threaten Kaydon properly."

CHAPTER TWENTY-FOUR

Kaydon

HE WAS SHOVING the last of the stuffed animals into a garbage bag, the balloons having already been deflated—or in the case of the giant Hello Kitty one, decapitated with his skate blade (with relish)—when Mandy walked into the room.

Fanny was at her shoulder.

And he knew he was in trouble.

One, this was a naked zone, dicks flopping all over the place as the guys showered and changed. They'd all spent a lifetime in locker rooms, years showering with other people, and even with Brit in the room, no one bothered much with modesty.

It was a *here a dick, there a dick, everywhere a dick, dick* mentality, and Old MacDonald was raising dicks on his farm, not ducks.

Brit—having played her whole life and seen her fair share of Old MacDonald's Dick Farm—didn't bat an eye.

Neither did Calle—their assistant coach—though she'd played women's hockey, and Kaydon tried to remember to wrap a towel around his particular dick field when she came in to discuss the game. But…nudity was just a part of the process.

Accepted. Ignored. Moving on.

All that being said, Mandy and Fanny coming into the locker room was unusual.

And boded of bad news.

More boding of that bad news? That they'd waited until the room cleared out and he was the only one left (fucking Hello Kitty) to come in.

Mandy had kids at home.

Fanny had classes to teach the next day and a fiancé warming her bed.

Most conversations could wait until they were at the practice facility in two days' time.

But not—apparently—this one. Because they came into the room, eyes scanning the interior, and then came straight over to him.

Mandy's expression was thunderclouds.

Fanny's wasn't much better, though he did notice that her mouth turned up when she noticed the plethora of Hello Kitty stuffed animals. "Do I want to ask?"

He glared. "I don't think you have to, not when you created this mess."

Her smile widened. "Kitten has claws."

He sighed, tied the top of the bag shut, and shrugged into his suit jacket. "I'm guessing you two aren't here to help me sweep up confetti?"

Mandy's eyes went wide. "There was confetti?" Her gaze left his, began scanning the skate mats. "There should *never* be confetti. What if it gets stuck to a skate blade? Someone might blow a tire and wipe out and hurt something and—"

She was protective.

He loved that about her.

Which is why he wasn't going to torment her.

"No confetti," he said. "It was a joke—"

Relief slid across her face. "A bad one."

Kaydon laughed softly. "Yes, a bad one." He stifled a sigh.

"No confetti, just plenty of balloons and printouts and stuffed animals. Oh! And a banner, too." He nodded at the bag he'd filled with trash. The stuffed animals he'd drop off at a donation center. They might as well go to some kids who would make use of them. "So," he said when quiet fell and neither one of them said anything. "What do I owe this illustrious visit to?"

"Sit," Fanny ordered.

"I'm fi—" He thought about arguing for a second. Then knew he'd just waste time and lose the argument anyway. He wanted to finish packing up and then go see Scar. She avoided the Old MacDonald Dick Farm at all costs, so he wasn't sure if she was still working or had packed it in and was waiting for him. Either way, he wanted to track her down, take her home, and fuck her until the sun came up.

So…he sat.

Mandy frowned as she sat on one side of him. Fanny did the same, though hers was more like a scowl, and sat on the other side.

Silence fell.

He absently rubbed his knee, didn't miss the pair of gazes that went there, and immediately drew his hand back.

Then he waited for them to speak.

They didn't.

And suddenly he was irritated. They'd cornered him in here when he was fine. He just wanted to get this conversation done as quickly as possible so he could get on with his evening. Get on with seeing Scar.

What he *didn't* want were some mental hoops he was going to have to leap through.

Spell it out. Get it done.

Get on with it.

"My knee is fine, okay?" he said and didn't miss the look they shot each other, the look that only served to further piss him off. "It's sore. Fuck"—he tossed his hands up—"it's always sore. But is it the type of injured, painful sore that got me surgery? No. Will I tell you when it is? Yes."

"Your stride tells me you're in pain," Fanny said, when he paused, chest heaving.

He sucked in a breath, strived for calm. Failed. Because though his voice was even, it was frosty enough to slice. "I *promised* you that I would come to you if it was the type of pain that I needed help managing, the type of pain that would fuck up my game. It's not. I don't know if you saw me play tonight, but I was on fire. I got a goal and two assists and didn't have to come off early once because it was bothering me."

"Fanny's not lying," Mandy said. "Your stride is off. I can tell you're playing in pain. We haven't even had our first regular season game yet. I can't clear you to play if you're only going to injure yourself again."

"My knee isn't hurting like that," he gritted. "I'm fine to play."

"So says the man who played through a torn ACL and MCL," Fanny pointed out.

A breath. "I appreciate the concern, but my knee is *fine*."

Silence.

Two women's stares boring into him.

And he knew that he'd only get this straightened out if he leveled with them. He'd been hoping to keep the thing between Scarlett and him quiet because the Gold gossip train was notorious, and if he thought he was getting shit for the *Kitten* nickname, it would be no amount of shit and teasing and "helping a man out" once the guys discovered he and Scar were together.

He tried one final time. "I promise you. My knee is fine."

Their determined looks didn't falter, and seriously, he loved them, appreciated their concern, respected the shit out of how they always went to bat for their players. *Always*. But right then he was really fucking annoyed.

"I'm fucking Scarlett, okay?" he snapped. "My entire body is sore because I'm sleeping with Scar and we're together and I'm helping her fix up her house. Is my knee tender? Yes. Is it because it's injured? No. Is it because we've been fucking like jackrabbits in between me completing her list of projects to get her home sorted out? Yes." He paused for a breath.

Mostly because they looked like kids who'd just been given free passes in a candy store.

Look, Billy. Here's Mommy's credit card. Buy all that you want.

"You and Scar?" Mandy asked.

He lifted his chin, glared, not sure he liked her tone. "Yeah. Me and Scar."

"And you're fixing up her house?" Fanny asked.

He turned, shifted his glare to her. "Yeah."

Fanny leaned around him. *Mandy* leaned around him.

Their stares locked.

And then they busted up laughing, long enough that he was ready to throttle the two of them, no matter how much he loved them. This was out of line. How dare they laugh at Scar? They were her friends. They were supposed—

"I told you," Mandy crowed. "Oh my God. I *told* you." She jumped up and did a little dance. "I knew there was something going on, knew that she liked you from the moment she knocked out that rack of sticks during the first photo shoot she coordinated. I knew it!" Turning, she plunked her hands on her hips and glared at Kaydon. "And you were convinced she didn't like you."

He kept his eyes on hers. "Kind of hard not to think that when a woman tries to run through all sorts of obstacles in order to avoid you."

"Obstacles—?" Fanny began then stopped, smacked her forehead. "I forgot about the garbage cans."

"And the delivery guy."

"And—"

"Enough," he said. "My point is that I got my head out of my ass, realized she wasn't running because she hated me. She was running because she liked me." He shrugged. "So, I did something about it."

"This is awesome!" Mandy fist-pumped.

"So awesome," Fanny said, putting up her hand for a high-five. "I just wish that I'd had something to do with the match-making instead of listening to that one"—she tilted her head at Mandy—"when she said that this would all work itself out, and to be patient."

Mandy huffed. "Well did it or didn't it work itself out?"

"Of course, it did," Fanny said. "I didn't even get to give you my talking to. *That's why* you've been avoiding me." She scowled. "I thought it was the drills."

He chuckled. "Well, it *was* the drills...and Scar."

Fanny made a face, her words belying her grouchiness. "She looks happy. *You* look happy, and I didn't even get to yell at anyone." She sighed. "*And* Mandy and I didn't get to be part of the matchmaking. *That's* always the best part."

"No one was a part of *your* little matchmaking story," Mandy pointed out. "All we knew was Brandon showed up on your porch and—bam!—you two were the ones being fuck bunnies."

"Hey!" Fanny said. "It wasn't *that* fast."

Kaydon smirked.

"We had a past," she said. "We just needed a little time to sort through that before..."

"You picked up where you'd left off?"

"Again. Not like *that.*"

"I can attest to that," Kaydon said. "She gave Brandon the runaround."

"See?" Fanny cried. "Kaydon got to be part of my match-making, and I didn't get to do anything but watch and wait and see with his." She pouted.

"The watching and waiting is the best part," Mandy said. "I've been around forever and can attest to *that.*"

"Maybe." A huff that told him she didn't really believe

Mandy before she turned back to him. "And now you're fixing up her house?"

He nodded, glad to finally be off the topic of matchmaking. "It's just small stuff." Minus the whole laundry room floor rebuilding thing—though in fairness, all he'd done for that was call in someone to fix it...and then argue with Scar about who was going to pay for it.

She'd won that one.

He'd won the garage door opener.

Victories. Small. Big. In between. He'd take all of them. He'd *also* take fighting with her. Because part of his body's soreness came from projects and part from fucking like rabbits and finally, a small part, from fucking like rabbits during makeup sex.

"Small stuff," Mandy repeated, and the concern slid back into her face.

"I'm done with most of the projects now," he said, and it was sort of the truth because between practices and travel, he wouldn't have as much time.

"Most." Another repeat. Another statement he could tell that Mandy didn't buy. "Can't you just hire someone?"

"Scar won't..." He trailed off, dropping that line of conversation because it wasn't their business.

"Won't let him pay for it," Fanny filled in, glancing around him at Mandy again. "How much do you want to bet that's the case?"

"No need for a bet. You *know* it's the case. She helps and helps but doesn't like to get any in return." Mandy locked eyes with him. "Did you know that Fanny and I tried to get her to let us paint her living room the last time we were over? She refused, plied us with margaritas until we forgot, and then sent us home sloshed in a Lyft. And she's been "too busy" getting ready for the season to have us over again." Mandy shot him a glare. "I'm guessing that's *your* doing?"

Since he couldn't deny that, he just said, "We've been busy."

She smirked.

"Also, her living room is painted."

That smirked widened. Fanny's joined in.

That lasted far too long for Kaydon's comfort, especially when the smirks were turned toward each other (or really the women turned their gazes, so they were looking at one another).

"So, your knee is fine," Mandy began slowly. "But you're looking wonky on the ice because the rest of you is sore."

"Right. I just need—" He frowned, processed the rest of the words. "Wonky? What the fuck, Mandy? I got a goal and two assists—"

Mandy didn't acknowledge him, nor did she look away from Fanny.

Who was calculating.

"Fuck no," he said, stepping back. "Whatever hellish drill just popped into your mind, there's no way that I'm doing it if it makes your face look like that."

She smiled.

It was pure evil.

Then she said, "I have an idea."

CHAPTER TWENTY-FIVE

Scar

SHE CLAMPED a hand over her chest as she crept away from the locker room.

You and Scar?

Laughter.

Laughter.

It still blared through her eardrums, still registered painfully through her veins.

You and Scar.

You.

And.

Scar.

Her eyes stung, and her heart felt shredded, and she thanked God that she'd just walked Charlie to his car, had bundled her brother up into his sedan and sent him on his way so he hadn't had to hear that, hadn't had to see her now.

God.

It *hurt*.

Mandy and Fanny were her friends.

And they thought the idea of her with Kaydon was laughable.

A tear slid down her cheek.

She shouldn't have stopped and listened when she heard the voices in the hallway. But when she'd heard Kaydon's, she thought about peeking in, seeing if she might be able to get him alone, and then once they were, to get on with realizing one of her fantasies—that being him fucking her against the wall where they had to be very quiet or else they might get caught.

That bit of naughtiness had vanished in an instant though.

Incredulity could do that to a woman.

You and Scar?

Fuck, why had Mandy had to say it like that? Why with so much surprise and…fuck, had there been disappointment in Mandy's voice? No. There couldn't be. Mandy liked her. She'd just pulled her aside the other day and complimented her latest contest for the Miner's Club—the youth program the Gold ran.

It wasn't disappointment.

It couldn't be.

But…what if it was?

She pushed into a bathroom and slammed the door behind her, flicking the lock before going over to the sink and bracing herself on it.

Sick. She literally felt sick, like she was going to lose everything she'd eaten up until that point in the day as she heaved and heaved and *heaved.*

Probably, she should be bending over the toilet instead.

But that might be dirty. Well, she was dirty. A dirty disappointment who—

A knock on the door before the handle tried to turn.

"Someone's in here," she croaked.

"Oh, sorry!" Mandy's voice penetrated the wood.

"Fuck," Scar breathed, looking at herself in the mirror, seeing the slightly swollen eyes, the red-tipped nose. What she would give to not be a redhead in that moment. A nice olive-colored skin would hide her flush, hide that reddened nose and eyes. But she was as white as she came, and there was no disguising it.

No running from it.

She flushed the toilet, made a production of washing her hands—which really was more about splashing water on her face in an effort to cool it down, to make that red go away.

She was pretty certain it didn't work, but at some point she had to stop pretend washing her hands and needed to go and face her friend.

Disappointment.

You and Scar?

A breath—long and slow in, long and slow out.

Because...*no.*

Hadn't she just had a conversation with her brother about putting the past in the past, about no longer viewing herself as a disappointment? Hadn't she said the reason she was beginning to put that aside was because of Kaydon? Because she wanted more with him?

So, what if Mandy and Fanny thought it was a joke?

Kaydon didn't; she was certain of it.

And he—well, she *and* he—were the only two that mattered.

She'd prove Mandy wrong, and she would tell that to her friend, straight up. No more hiding and crying. No more worrying about drama. She wanted Kaydon, and she was going to fight for it.

"Right," she whispered. "You're going to look Mandy in the eyes, and you're going to tell her to take that laugh and fuck right off to Fanny." A nod. "And then you're going to tell *both* of them to eff right off down the road because you don't need friends who don't want the best for you."

Another nod.

Another, "Right."

A deep breath in, letting it out.

She dried her hands, opened the door, and…stared into the empty hallway.

Mandy was gone.

———

SHE DID, ultimately, return to the locker room, and this time it was to find Kaydon alone.

He was coming out of the door with two huge garbage bags in his hands.

One he lugged to the garbage can in the hall and dropped it inside. The other he tossed over his shoulder, turned, and…

His smile hit her like an arrow to the heart.

Not a disappointment.

When he looked at her like that, she knew that she wasn't one. Not in his eyes. And that bolstered her own supports, her own determination to not see herself like that again.

"Hey, sweetcheeks," he said, dropping the bag and closing the distance between them. He brushed her hair out of her face, and his expression faltered, concern taking its place. "What's wrong?" he asked.

She shook her head. "Nothing."

"Not nothing"—he swept his thumb beneath one eye and then the other, and for a moment she thought that he knew she'd been crying—"there are shadows here, Scar. Tension"—he swept his thumb over the corners of her mouth—"here. So, what's up?"

Shadows and tension were better than tear-stained cheeks.

"Charlie's back," she said, going for diversion.

He stilled. "I thought he was supposed to be away for a while yet."

"He was. Something happened, but he won't tell me what it is." Kaydon frowned and concern rippled across his face. Warmth bubbled up inside her at the show, at his next words.

"We'll find out, sweetcheeks," he promised, wrapping her in

his arms and tugging her close. He smoothed a hand up and down her spine, and she couldn't help but melt. God, she loved it when he did that. "We'll make sure he's good, and if he's not, we'll get him there."

That warmth spread.

Because he was concerned in the first place. Because he'd said *we'll*. Because he was extending his care and protection and love to her brother.

The one person in her family who was alive to care for *her*. Not appearances or what he might get out of her. Just Scar. Just a woman who was trying to do better, make a better life, and who wouldn't let her past get to her any longer.

It occurred to her then that Kaydon hadn't laughed at what Mandy and Fanny said.

He hadn't commented, either.

But...she hadn't stuck around long enough to be certain of that fact. Maybe he hadn't interrupted the laughing but had straightened them out afterward. Maybe that's why Mandy had disappeared? Because she felt guilty about laughing and Kaydon had given her the business.

Business being...letting her friends know this thing between them was real and not a joke and—

God.

She was spiraling again.

She should have stayed and listened to the full conversation. She shouldn't have delayed talking to Mandy and telling her how she felt. She should have walked into the fucking locker room, kissed Kaydon within an inch of his life, and then turned to the women and said, "You got a problem with me, eh?"

Spiraling.

Taking a deep breath, she stifled her inner gangster, put a giant Stop sign up in front of the spiraling, and lifted her chest up from where she'd rested it against Kaydon's torso.

His gorgeous brown eyes met hers, the depths soft and still laced with concern.

"He's mad at me," she blurted.

A frown drawing his features together. "Why is Charlie mad at you?"

She touched his cheek, traced lightly over a slight scrape he must have earned on the ice. "Because he says that he's neither big or strong enough to properly threaten you to treat me right."

Kaydon froze.

And then he did the best thing ever, he laughed. Loudly and freely, and the sound filled her up, almost to bursting, lifting her out of the dredges of that spiral, pushed down the hurt, the worry of being a failure and disappointment.

It set her on her feet, steady and with renewed sureness.

She'd talk to Fanny, to Mandy.

Explain that she'd heard and hated it, give them a chance to express their concerns, and then tell them to back right the fuck off her and Kaydon.

She wouldn't internalize this anymore.

She wouldn't hurt silently.

She wouldn't—

Kaydon's laughter cut off, his hand lifting to cup her cheek. "My precious girl," he whispered. "So fucking beautiful and fierce." He dragged his thumb across her mouth, across what must be a frown between her brows. "Don't worry," he said. "I'll handle your brother."

She pushed away her thoughts, focused on the man in front of her.

"Charlie's stronger than you give him credit for."

"Of course, he is," Kay said, not missing a beat, the words warm and quick and without any hesitation. "He has you for a sister, doesn't he? He couldn't learn to be anything *but* strong."

CHAPTER TWENTY-SIX

Kaydon

He smiled as he slipped into bed two weeks later.

Scar had left the light on for him, and sitting in front of it was the tiny Hello Kitty he'd snagged from the bag just before he'd dropped the rest of them off at the donation center.

Four or five inches tall, it had been on the top shelf of his locker, tucked away so he'd barely seen it—probably to be resurrected in order to torment Kaydon at a later date. He'd liked the idea of hiding it for Scar to find while he was out on a road trip, so he'd left it under her pillow when he'd gone out of town the week before.

Then texted her to say he was in her bed.

She'd texted back to say her bed was empty.

(A good thing since he wasn't there to warm it).

He'd texted back telling her to check under the pillow.

The small stuffed toy had been discovered, she'd called him with laughter and love in her voice, and the stuffy had made itself a permanent home in front of her lamp.

Staring at her while she slept.

More of his excellent creepiness skills, she'd teased.

He grinned, thinking of the text she'd sent saying that *Kitten* was going to have to find a home if he didn't stop staring, and her pert reply when he'd said he *liked* staring.

The toy had kept up his watch.

And now he was home.

Normally, Scar came on the longer road trips, but when the team flew out for a game or two, she tended to stay at the home base, catching up on tasks, handling things Rebecca used to cover but now was turning over to Scar as she transitioned to part-time.

So, Scar hadn't flown out yet.

He hoped, though, that she was coming on next week's long trip. The team would be gone for nearly two weeks and would be playing in Minnesota. His parents were coming to that game. He wanted Scar to be there, to meet them, to—

"Kay," she murmured, her eyes closed, still asleep but rolling over and burrowing her way into his arms.

She did that every time he came home.

He fucking loved it.

Loved *her*.

Especially when she took her time burrowing in then folded her hands beneath her chin, buried her face in his throat, and fell fully back asleep.

Her hair tickled his jaw every time. Her breath was hot on his skin. His arms always went numb.

He didn't give a fuck.

Because *she* was in them.

Closing his eyes, he let sleep take him under.

———

THE KNOCK TOOK him by surprise.

Partly because it hadn't come on the front door, but mostly because he'd been so engrossed in the book in his lap that he hadn't heard anyone approach.

Hadn't registered footsteps.

Barely registered the figure leaning on the door.

Until she spoke.

"Hi, baby," Scar said, moving into the room. She had on tight black leggings with little gray boots that hit her at the ankle, a sweater that covered up way too much, but at least was form-fitting enough to show off those gorgeous tits of hers. Unfortunately, she also had a scarf draped around her neck, hiding most of them (acceptable so the rest of the male populace couldn't see, deplorable because *he* couldn't see them). Tiny pumpkin earrings dangled from her ears, and she had on minimal makeup—exactly the way he preferred so that he could see *her*. Beautiful Scar who had been working her butt off since that morning.

Rebecca had pulled her into a project almost before dawn, and since he'd crawled into her bed barely two hours before then, he hadn't exactly been ready to face the day.

She'd tucked him in, closed the bedroom door, and worked until he'd stumbled out of bed.

Upon which she'd pointed to the coffee pot, he'd indulged in the black brew until he felt human enough to eat (delivery from Molly's—thank God it was a Cheat Day...then again, *of course* Scar remembered it was a Cheat Day).

Since her project—a PR overhaul of the Rush (now *that* was a job and a half)—had no sign of slowing, he'd left her to it, telling her to come over any time.

It was now—he glanced at his watch—six in the evening, he'd been reading for the last six hours, and his woman was there. Walking in on him reading erotica (which, again, he'd washed his mind out with bleach to forget it had once belonged to his mother and focused on the fact that Scar liked it and he wanted to understand what she liked). It was also why he was sporting a chub.

Because he was imagining doing all the things in the book with the sexy redhead walking toward him.

"Dinner," he rasped, closing the book and shoving it into the cushion.

She paused and he cleared his throat, ignoring the way she tilted her head curiously. "What are you reading, KayKay?"

He grinned because he thought it was funny when she did that, when she called him KayKay. He also grinned because she liked his smile and he was trying to distract her and...right, she was coming closer, which meant he had to act. Now.

He stood, moved toward her, meeting her a few feet away from the chair, sweeping her up into his arms and laying a kiss on her that he knew would reduce her to mush.

When he pulled back—his heart thrumming, feeling very much like mush himself—he cupped her cheek, weaved his fingers into her hair. "You tired, sweetcheeks?" he asked, gently massaging her scalp and using his other hand to straighten her glasses.

"No," she murmured, and let her body fall against his.

Then she kissed *him*, reduced him to something mushier than mush—slime dripping down onto carpet, a soda exploding in the heat of a car, a Popsicle melting under the sun.

"I—"

She didn't break off for once to gather her thoughts. Instead, she broke off as she left his slime-filled, burst soda can, popsicle puddle self those couple of feet away from the chair and launched herself toward it, shoving her hand down between the back and the cushion and—

"I knew it!" she exclaimed, holding the book up like it was a trophy.

And hell, for the ideas it had given him, he was half-convinced it should be gilded and mounted on the wall in some museum somewhere.

Read this, men. Read this and learn.

A simple inscription. But effective.

And poignant.

And...the cat was out of the bag.

She opened the book to where he'd been writing in the margins, taking notes because he wasn't dumb and she liked the books, and...that shit was hot, so he was adding everything to his long list of things he wanted to do with her.

He'd need five lifetimes to fuck her in every way he imagined.

Hence the need for a list and writing in margins.

He'd color code that shit and make his way through it.

Her lips moved as her eyes went wide. "You're actually reading it," she whispered. "And taking notes."

"I mean"—he rubbed the back of his neck, his cheeks going hot—"you said you liked it. I...um...wanted to read it, and then I realized"—a shrug—"I like it, too. I thought...well, I thought we could try some things from it, from *them*."

Heat in those pale blue eyes, a flush spreading out along her cheeks, down along her jaw. "Them?"

A whisper.

Well, hell, he'd really shown his hand now.

"Them," he confirmed because...in for a penny, in for a pound.

Her cheeks went redder, but not because she was embarrassed.

He knew her blushes now. Knew the ones that came from being upset, from spiraling—thankfully few and far between now. He knew the ones that were because she was angry—usually spouting off about some asshole on the other team who'd dared hurt him (he liked her when she was fired up on his behalf). And he knew the ones that flared on those pretty cheeks because she was turned on.

That was today's.

It was desire.

Desire that had him determinedly striding toward her—which, thankfully, didn't take long because he was still close to the chair. He swept her up into his arms, started to carry her out of the room, to the stairs, to his bed because...well, because of obvious reasons.

The biggest one of which was prodding her through the fabric of his jeans.

"KayKay?" she asked.

"Hmm?" he replied, burying his face in that scarf in search of skin and finding...sweater.

Ugh.

She tugged lightly at his hair, held up the book to a page he'd pretty much written an essay to in the margins, and asked, "Can we try this one?"

CHAPTER TWENTY-SEVEN

Scar

HIS EYES SCANNED the page and then returned to hers, a wicked grin spreading on his face.

Heat in deep brown eyes, strong arms clenching around her, his spiced scent filling her nose.

"This one?" he asked, fingers digging into her hips. "You sure?"

"Am I sure I want you to strip me naked and fuck me on one of these shelves?" she asked, heart pounding and with far more confidence than was probably good for her, given how *good* Kaydon was at fucking her.

She'd be fucked limp.

She'd be pleasured into near unconsciousness.

She'd be...ready and willing and so damned glad she had him in her life, that he cared enough about the things she liked to read the books, to make notes, to want to explore.

With her.

With. *Her.*

That realization had the last of her self-doubt sliding away. She'd been barricading it up, ignoring it, forcing herself to not give it time or space in her thoughts, but it had still been lingering…just there on the edges, waiting to pounce.

But…he'd read the books.

He'd taken notes.

He'd shown up, been present, not flinched when her parents tried their bullshit, and he hadn't brought an ounce of drama into her life or work.

It was time to unclip that final safety belt and fly free.

"Yes, sweetcheeks," he said, nipping her bottom lip and striding back over to the chair. "You want me to strip you naked and fuck you on one of these"—he dropped her onto the cushion, swept an arm out to encompass the room—"shelves?"

Smiling, she wound her arms around him and held tight. "Yes, please."

A growl that had goose bumps prickling on her skin, heat arrowing down her spine, her knees going watery, and her pussy…

Wet.

She was so damned wet already.

"Good," he said, and nipped her lips again, and then her jaw, and her earlobe, and her throat. His stubble rubbed against her, prickling her skin, making it beyond sensitive, and probably leaving marks that the team would tease her about tomorrow…if they saw them.

Well, good thing it was scarf season—

Speaking of, he yanked the pale orange infinity scarf she had draped around her neck, threw it to the side. "I hate these fucking things," he grumbled, tugging the neckline of her sweater down, pressing his mouth to her skin. Nipping and kissing and tonguing his way toward her breasts.

"My scarf?" she asked breathlessly.

"Yes." Another grumble. Another nip, this time on the top of her breast, making her cry out, streams of pleasure exploding through her.

"Why?" she managed to gasp out, just before he reared back

and yanked her sweater over her head, exposing her breasts. His hot gaze went to hers and slowly slid south, an almost tangible touch as it drifted over her mouth, her throat, her breasts.

He made her feel like her pale blue cotton bra was the sexiest lingerie.

He made her feel like *she* was the sexiest woman *no matter* what she was wearing.

He made her—

Naked.

He made her naked. While she was processing the warm and fuzzy that went along with his hot gaze, Kaydon was much more productive. He sat back on his heels, yanked off one of her boots. Then the other.

Then reached for her leggings, and…

Voila!

The man had magically gotten her naked.

Her bra went one way. Her panties—along with her leggings —another. One boot landed upright on a shelf. The other arced dangerously close to the lamp.

Then she was bare.

He was fully clothed.

Except for his feet. Those were as bare as she was, peeking out from beneath the jeans he was wearing.

Kaydon reached for his shirt, started to tug it up and over his head.

"Wait," she said.

"Mmm?"

He seemed to get distracted, bending over to suckle at one breast, to flick the nipple on her other breast, sending liquid pooling in her pussy, dampening the tops of her thighs. Yeah, she was ready for him. Ready and needy and—

He reached for his shirt again.

She remembered why she'd stopped him.

Normally, she loved that sexy body, wanted it on full display.

Today…she wanted to reenact the book.

"Wait," she said again, grabbing hold of his hand, staying the motion. "He stays clothed, remember?" she asked. "He stays clothed and she's not and—"

Wicked intent. Scorching heat.

His hand tugged free of hers, and he hefted her up, cradling her against his chest and bringing her across the room and perching her onto a shelf.

He reached between them, his knuckles brushing against her pussy as he flicked open the button on his jeans and pulled out his cock. His pants slipped just beneath his hips, caught on his thighs. His cock was hard and gleaming with precum, ready for her.

Ready to pound into her.

"Is this what you want, sweetcheeks?" he rasped, dragging it up through her folds.

"Oh, God," she breathed, dropping her head back. "Oh. My. God."

He pulled back, nipped her nose. "Is. This. What. You. *Want?*"

Oh. God.

Fuck, yes. That's what she wanted.

He grinned, and she realized she'd spoken aloud, but she couldn't be embarrassed, not with the wolfish expression, not with the heat on his face, not with his hard cock…

Pressing into her.

Oh. God. *Again.*

Her head dropped back, plunked against the shelf above her.

"Sweetcheeks," he murmured as he slipped his hand behind her head, cradling her skull, protecting her, even like this.

Her pussy convulsed.

He groaned, hips jerking, cock pulsing inside her.

"Fuck me, Kaydon," she groaned, wrapping her thighs around his waist, her fingers digging into his biceps.

"Working." A hard thrust that had the shelf creaking. "On." Another that had books tumbling to the ground like giant, heavy pieces of confetti. "It." One more.

The shelf collapsed.

But Kaydon had her.

She didn't even experience one moment of feeling like she was going to fall, of gravity taking her over. He just stepped away from the mess, perched her on another shelf, and continued fucking her even as more books fell, as that shelf creaked ominously, as—

"Oh fuck!" she cried. "That's it—right—*oh God oh God oh God!*"

She came, diving beneath the surface of her pleasure, drowning in it, her vision going black, her body tensing and then feeling as though it didn't belong to her as she sank and sank and *sank*.

When she finally came to, little aftershocks of pleasure scouring through her, it was to find them on the ground with Kaydon holding her against his chest, his hard cock still inside her, his arms wrapped tight. They were both breathing heavily, and she thought she might be sweating all over a copy of *Jurassic Park*. Somehow it had gotten pinned between them.

But she didn't think the dinos would mind.

What she and Kaydon had done was classic prehistoric fucking.

"Bingo! Dino DNA."

The line from the movie trailed through her mind, and she giggled.

Bingo! Dino *fucking*.

She giggled again.

Kaydon's arms tightened. "I hope you're not laughing at my erotica pleasuring skills."

She pulled back enough to point at the shelves, at the books, at the novel under her right thigh. She tugged it out. "How about your dino erotica pleasuring skills?"

His gaze went to the book then to her face.

His expression had been lined with humor, but when he stared into her eyes, his own grew serious—serious enough that a pit opened in her stomach. Then he lifted his hand, gently cupped her jaw. "God, I love you."

And she melted against him. "I love you, Kaydon," she whispered against his chest.

His arms tightened. "Now," he said, kissing the top of her head. "I demand an explanation of dino erotica."

A pat to the yummy muscles there. "Don't worry, I'll recommend some books."

CHAPTER TWENTY-EIGHT

Kaydon

HE'D JUST OPENED his mouth to ask what in the fuck all she meant by *I'll recommend some books*, when the doorbell rang.

She jumped.

He kissed the top of her head again.

"Just ignore it," he said, his cock stirring already. "I have more notes about that book."

"The dino porn book?"

Kay chuckled as he shook his head. "No, sweetcheeks, about that scene in the library where he bends her over the—"

The doorbell rang again.

Only this time, it was accompanied by Scar's phone ringing.

She went stiff, her head coming up off his chest, contrition written into every delicate feature. "Um…" she began.

And he knew he wasn't getting any bending her over the card catalog.

Not that he had a card catalog or was even sure if *libraries* still had them (probably not since everything was digitized), but he'd find one. He vowed it upon the game-used stick he had tucked away at the top of his closet.

"What, sweetcheeks?" he asked.

"I kind of...um...I kind of forgot that I invited Charlie over to make dinner for us."

The doorbell went again. Scar's phone cut off ringing then immediately started up again. "You invited your brother to my house...to cook for us?"

Scar winced. "I should have asked you first. It's just that he's a little lonely, and Fanny and Brandon were busy, and he was making his special homemade ravioli, and I *love* his ravioli, and since he was already going to make it at his house, I figured he could make it here because you have a really nice kitchen and it's really awesome to cook in and—"

He'd realized that she thought he was upset about inviting Charlie over about the second *and* in.

"Scar," he interrupted before she could add any more *and*s. "I'm not mad that he's here. I'm just not used to having guests cook for me in my house. It's...well, suffice to say if my mom were here right now, she'd be smacking me on the back of the head and demanding that I treat him as a guest should be treated."

Relief slid through her face. "I...you're not mad."

He shook his head. "Not mad."

She nibbled at her bottom lip. "I meant to tell you."

He helped her to her feet and then whipped off his shirt, used it to wipe them both up before tugging up his jeans and handing Scar her clothes. "My mom would also be smacking me for leaving a guest on the porch," he said lightly as he buttoned and zipped up. He pressed a kiss to her lips as her phone rang for the third time. "I'll go let him in, get him settled in the kitchen, and then go upstairs for a fresh shirt. You get dressed and come out when you're ready."

Scar nodded, on board with the plan, but then her eyes went wide as she took in the devastation from their little library fucking reenactment (and really, she should remove the word *little* from that description).

"But what about—" Here she faltered, just swept a hand out, encompassing that devastation with a gesture.

"We'll do what I did when I was a kid and my brother and I hadn't cleaned our room even though guests were coming over and we should have."

Her brows lifted.

His voice dropped to a conspiratorial whisper. "We shut the door."

A giggle, her lips tipping up. "I can do that."

"Good."

He headed for the door, stopped when she called, "Kay?"

"Yeah, sweetcheeks?"

"I love you."

Three words.

Not little. Not in the least.

———

THE RAVIOLIS WERE *ALMOST* worth the interruption.

Almost.

"These are incredible," he murmured, thanking all that was holy that Charlie coming over had fallen on a Cheat Day.

If there was ever proof that there was a God, Kay had gotten it today.

"Thanks," Charlie said, and though he was a decent-sized guy, he hadn't made much of a dent in his pasta. In fact, he hadn't made much of a dent in anything he'd cooked that evening. Not the stuffed mushrooms or the spinach salad, not the bread.

And not the ravioli with roasted asparagus.

Paired with dark circles and pale skin, wrinkled clothes, and mismatched socks, and…Kaydon was worried.

He'd met the other man a few times during Gold events—though that had always been under the context of Fanny's friend or Scar's brother. Unlike tonight, which was strictly under the guise of concerned brother making sure his sister's boyfriend was up to snuff. And he was doing a good job of making Kay feel like he was under scrutiny, making him uncertain if he'd pass muster.

(As a brother himself, Kaydon could appreciate that Charlie had mastered those skills)

But aside from the narrowed eyes and obvious judgment, there was something that Charlie was hiding—a pain he'd tried to shove down and bury. It was in the pale skin, the dark circles, the wrinkled clothes, and mismatched socks. Kay hadn't ever gotten the impression that Scar's brother was obsessed with the way he looked, but Charlie had always been put together, impeccably groomed.

And the circles hadn't been there.

It could be jet lag. After all, the man *had* returned from South Korea not too long before.

But Kaydon knew enough about jet lag to know that it shouldn't be going on *this* long.

Sick, maybe? Had picked up a bug over there?

Kay supposed that could be true, but it didn't seem likely, not when Charlie appeared hale and hearty—minus those circles and pale skin.

So that got him thinking. About pain and hiding it and how that seemed to be an Andrews' trait. Burying old hurts so they could pretend they didn't exist. So, while he didn't think Charlie's pain was exactly like Scar's—her insecurities from her parents, fear of disappointing people who loved her because her mother and father were such giant tool bags— Kaydon did know it had to play a factor. And he worried it was something big, something that Charlie was suffering with.

Would continue to suffer with.

He had the feeling that Charlie wouldn't talk to him about it—they hardly knew each other and unleashing brotherly protective skills didn't automatically open a channel to spilling their guts. But more than that, he wasn't sure he'd talk to Scar or even Fanny, who he'd become close with, about it.

Charlie was too good at deflecting the conversation away from himself, redirecting it to others.

And he showed his skills in that area all through the rest of dinner, through washing the dishes—though Kaydon had drawn the line at Charlie helping with them since the other man had cooked him a three-course meal in his own house. Which meant *Kaydon* had done the dishes while refilling Charlie and Scar's wineglasses as they talked about his plans for staying in the Bay Area.

Apparently, his lease was coming up, and though he'd gotten lucky because his sublet tenet had wanted to break their contract early and move in with her boyfriend, thus freeing the space back up to Charlie, he needed to decide if he was going to continue to live there.

"My company offered me a position at the New York office," he said as he served them up dessert—tiramisu, thank you Jesus. "But I like being here, so I may just take some time and look for something so that I can stay here."

"I'd like you to be close," Scar said, "but..." She trailed off, nibbled on her bottom lip, and then shoved a giant bite of dessert into her mouth.

"Do I have enough savings?" Charlie asked gently.

Scar winced.

Charlie patted her hand. "I'm good," he said. "I haven't touched anything from Heath—or not much of it anyway—and I got a good severance from my company."

Severance?

Even as they offered another position?

Kaydon smelled something fishy going on.

But...not his brother.

Just Scar's and her only decent family. Which meant that Charlie had now become incredibly important to Kaydon.

"You can always stay here," he blurted during a pause in conversation as he washed up the dessert dishes.

Charlie set down his wine glass, turned slowly, his eyes wide, and he stared at Kaydon. "You want me." A beat. "To stay." Another. "Here?"

"Well, if your lease is up, and you want to remain in the area." He shrugged and returned to doing the dishes. "It's not like I don't have space. Plus," he added, "it would be nice to have someone around when I'm out of town…"

There was such complete silence that he turned around again.

Charlie and Scar were both staring at him with wide eyes.

"What?" he asked.

Charlie didn't answer him directly. Just glanced at Scar and said, "He's serious."

Scar nodded. "Yes."

"He's the real thing."

Half of Scar's mouth tipped up.

"He loves you."

"I know." The other half of her mouth joined the first. "And I love him."

Charlie brushed his fingers over that beautiful curve, the one Kaydon had begun living for. "I'm so happy for you, sissy." He reached over and hugged her tightly. "And even more happy that you were able to welcome it into your life."

Kay tried to slip from the room, thinking that he would give brother and sister some time to talk, give them their moment, which would hopefully be followed up by Scar having a chance to wrestle whatever demons were wreaking havoc with Charlie out of him, but just as he made it to the hall, Charlie pulled back.

"Hey, you!" he called.

Kaydon slid to a stop.

"Get in here," Charlie ordered.

Kay glanced at Scar, who was tucked into Charlie's chest, at

Charlie, whose eyes were a little damp, but who was clearly happy for his sister…and who clearly wouldn't be spilling his guts that evening.

So, he got in there.

Walked right into Charlie's free—and extended—arm and got in on the brother/sister group hug.

Then he figured that since he was already in, since Charlie was now his—albeit in a different way than Scar was his, but still his to watch out for, another brother to protect—he said, "Or we could finish up Scar's guest bedroom, and you can move in there." They both stilled. "Or maybe you could just go straight into the master and kick Scar out."

Scar leaned back. "And where would I go?"

"Here," he said. Then shrugged. "Or Charlie could come here, and I could go there."

Wide eyes.

A blush creeping onto her cheeks.

"Kay," she breathed in that melty way that had his cock doing things it really should *not* be doing, especially in such close contact to her brother.

Being on the snide.

His knee hurting.

Fanny's torturous drills.

The quick succession of thoughts tempered the reaction.

And it disappeared altogether, was replaced by laughter when Charlie said, "There. It's settled. You guys are going to Scar's place."

"Why?" Scar asked, sounding affronted.

"Why?" Charlie dropped his arms then swept one toward the kitchen window, where the outlines of the sauna and hot tub area were visible thanks to his exterior lights and a timer. "*Why?* Seriously, sis, have you not seen that hot tub?"

Scar froze, cheeks flaring.

Kaydon froze.

Scar recovered first. "Yeah, LiLi," she said, going for casual and failing miserably. "I've seen the hot tub."

Charlie studied her face.

Then pretended to gag.

"And note to self, buy a gallon of bleach for said hot tub before partaking."

Kay snorted. Scar giggled.

Then all started busting up.

Even Charlie.

They might not have discovered exactly what was bothering him, but he was laughing and with family and...that was a start.

CHAPTER TWENTY-NINE

Scar

"So, how about a tour of my new place?" Charlie asked as he shrugged into his coat. "I mean, I already got a glimpse of the hot tub—"

"And sauna," Kaydon said.

The stink was trying to make her blush.

The stink *was* making her blush.

"Also picking up bleach wipes for the sauna, apparently," Charlie said dryly.

Scar's cheeks heated further, but she lifted her chin and said, "That's none of your business." She pointed down the hall. "You've already seen the kitchen and the front porch."

Charlie snorted.

"And the hot tub," she went on determinedly.

"Bleach," Charlie deadpanned.

"There's the dining room," she began, and wondered why in the hell she was giving the tour when it was Kaydon's house. But he just seemed content to sit back and watch her suffer. They both did. Men. Evil beings, they were.

Yoda, she was.

"And this is Kaydon's office," she said after Charlie gave the dining room the cursory glance she expected him to give.

Her brother may be very organized and dress well and have a neatly decorated apartment, but he had zero patience for home goods. When he'd moved into his place, he'd hit Target up, gotten what he needed to fulfill his vision in under an hour, and had gotten the hell out.

She, on the other hand, had gone to all the big box stores, shopped online, visited several furniture stores, and then gone *back* to the big box stores—to Target—and had spent half a day filling her cart with throw pillows.

Just throw pillows.

That was the last time Charlie had shopped with her.

Probably for the best.

"Oh, damn," Charlie said. "That's a nice TV."

"For all the *office* work he does in here," she teased, nodding to the video game console sitting beneath the TV.

"Of course, it is," Charlie said, not missing a beat. "Got to exercise those hands...and, yikes, I'm going to stop myself right there."

"Yes," Kay said softly, sweeping her hair off her nape and pressing a kiss there, "I've got to exercise my hands." He trailed one down her spine as Charlie wandered out of the room, squeezing one cheek through her leggings and reminding her that she hadn't been able to find her underwear earlier. Hadn't been able to find it before she had just ended up closing the door like Kaydon had suggested.

The door...Charlie was walking toward.

Because he'd turned right.

Because he'd moved down the hall...toward it.

And right on cue, he called, "Is this one of those hidden bookcases? Scar has always wanted one of those." Laughter. "No wonder you're dating him, Scar. It's like he's got your Pinterest board printed in his brain."

Oh shit.

Oh. *Shit.*

He—

She jumped away from Kaydon, sprinted out into the hall. "LiLi, wait!"

Her brother had his hand on a book—on fucking *Game of Thrones* (because of course he did!)—and was tugging it forward. "What Scar?" he asked, unlocking the door, pushing it wide. "Is this like a secret sex dungeon instead of a hidden library?" He glanced over his shoulder, a grin spreading across his face. "Kaydon, do you have a Red Room? Should I take my sister and get her far, far from your palace of sin?" He turned away, started to step into the room then stopped, his mouth falling open. "Christ. Did a bomb go off in here?"

Scar lurched toward him. "I—"

He leaned forward, grabbed something. A book, she realized when he spun toward them and held it up. With something on top of it. Her cheeks flared as he asked with barely restrained humor, "Any reason there are panties draped across *Gulliver's Travels?*"

Hot cheeks. So fucking hot, she had to be fire engine red. "He's a man well-traveled?" she attempted.

"I don't think that's exactly what the book is about," Charlie whispered.

She grabbed the book—and the panties—from her brother, tossed the book onto the nearest shelf, crumpled the panties into her hand. "It doesn't matter. Let's get on with the tour—"

Crack.

She screeched and jumped.

Gulliver's Travels had apparently proved to be too much for the shelf because it collapsed, sending another whole load of books tumbling down onto the floor.

When they'd stopped falling, Charlie turned from the devastation, wide-eyed. "I think it's safer that I move into Scar's place." A beat. "Less bleach required."

"No, there's not," she and Kaydon said at the same time.

Slowly, she spun toward him, amusement boiling up inside her, taking the place of embarrassment.

Because Kay's eyes were dancing.

Charlie gagged.

She laughed, couldn't stop. Laughed so hard she bent at the waist and had to brace her hands on her thighs.

Kay grinned, bent with her, and nipped her ear. "Fuck, I love you, sweetcheeks."

He'd said those words a lot, was free with them, never made her work for them. No strings. Just gave them, easy and loose.

But that didn't mean they meant any less, didn't change the way her heart squeezed when he gave them to her, how the coldness that had been inside her for so long had been defrosted, warmed through, packed in a scarf and mittens and given a space heater.

Because he gave them so freely, they meant *more.*

They meant everything.

Even more so because she could give them to him right back.

"WHAT DO you think of this one?" Mandy asked, holding up a jacket.

Since it was cute, a mix of lace and leather and fit Mandy's spunky personality—and the nice date outfit she was trying to pick out for her and Blane's anniversary—Scar nodded. "I think it's perfect."

"Yes!" Fanny exclaimed and moved over to another rack, snagging up a tight black dress that appeared to be more lace than actual dress. Sexy, skimpy, perfect for the date night. "And then you can wear it over this. Blane's going to lose his shit."

Mandy glanced from the dress down to her body. "I can't wear that," she said, smoothing a hand over her stomach. "I'm so fat still from the baby. My stomach—"

"Is beautiful," Fanny said. "Because it carried two babies, and its—"

"Saggy," Mandy muttered.

Scar didn't like to hear her friend sound so insecure, but she understood it. *God* knew that she understood it.

"Just try it on," she coaxed. "Blane is going to love to see you get dressed up, and you know that he loves your body."

Mandy pressed her lips together. "I know. He always says he'd love me in a paper bag. I just—"

"Wish that things were different?" she finished when Mandy cut herself off. "Wish you could change things about yourself?" She gave a chagrined smile. "Tell me about it. There are a whole host of things I'd *love* to change about myself. Despite Kaydon saying how much he loves me."

Fanny frowned. "Why? You're great, Scar."

She made a face, flipped through a rack, almost wishing she hadn't brought this up, even though she knew that she needed to. As much as she'd tried to push it out of her head, it had been eating at her over the last weeks. She should have probably just mentioned it to Kay, talked it out with him. But…his reaction wasn't the one she was worried about.

It was her friends'.

She'd been pretending she hadn't eavesdropped, hadn't overheard their reactions, but she didn't want to be that person.

She'd figured out who she was with a man who really loved her, who treated her as she deserved.

She could figure it out with her friends, make sure those friends are ones that were the same.

Not a disappointment.

A valuable component.

Which was why instead of changing the subject, she blurted out, "Well, if I'm so great, then you wouldn't have laughed hysterically when Kaydon told you we were dating."

Silence fell between the three of them.

Hell, it almost seemed like it fell in the entire department store.

Moisture burned the backs of her eyes, and she glanced away, blinked rapidly, searched the racks in case there was a better dress for Mandy's date.

A gentle hand peeled hers from the death grip she had on the hanger of a truly horrific, ruffled, puke green monster of a dress. "No one should be subjected to that," Fanny whispered.

"No one," Mandy agreed, wrapping an arm around Scar's waist.

The three of them stood like that for a moment before Mandy led them to a bench on the far side of the space, tucked into the wall between the bathrooms and the dressing rooms. Once there, they coaxed Scar into sitting between them.

"Why do you think we laughed?" Mandy asked carefully.

Scar sighed, scooted forward enough to dislodge Mandy's arm, withdrew her hand, and placed it in her lap so that she was self-contained, so that she wasn't relying on—

A breath.

Forcing herself to scoot back, to meet each of their eyes in turn. "I heard you," she said evenly. "I was coming to find Kaydon, and I heard him tell you we were dating. Heard him say it, and then I heard you two..." A breath, slowly in, slowly out. "I heard you two roar with laughter. I mean, I know that I'm not the obvious choice for him. I know that I can be klutzy and a mess and—and"—she shoved her glasses up her nose, perilously close to tears—"I know that my glasses never stay where they're supposed to!"

Mandy opened her mouth.

She kept talking. "But I also know that I love him, and he loves me and that I've had enough people in my life who've made me feel like shit and a disappointment and who always took their humor at my expense." She took another breath, released it slowly. "I don't want people in my life like that anymore. I'm more than that. I deserve more than that."

Her heart was pounding.

Tears still threatened.

But she forced herself to meet each of their gazes, to hold them so they knew she meant business. She loved these women, but she wasn't lying. She couldn't do it anymore. She needed *more*.

Mandy dropped a hand onto her arm. "I agree with everything you just said, honey." She squeezed lightly. "But, Scar, you didn't actually ask us *why* we were laughing."

Scar froze, realization hitting home.

She *hadn't* asked.

"Because if you had," Mandy said gently, "you would have known that our"—she glanced at Fanny, who nodded—"laughter was of the *I told you so* variety. As in"—another squeeze—"I told Kaydon that you two were perfect for each other approximately three weeks after he joined the team."

"I think it was the day of the stick incident," Fanny murmured.

"No," Scar said. "That was later." She sighed, dropped her head into her hands for a moment before straightening again... because facing things straight on. "I think it was the time I accidentally knocked the Miner down the stairs."

Fanny winced. "Right. I'd forgotten about that."

"I, unfortunately, haven't," Scar muttered.

Mandy nudged her. "Served that scary bastard right."

"Goldie isn't much better," Scar said, still muttering. But it was less because she'd had her feelings hurt and more because she could *not* believe that *one* preseason game with the unfortunate mascot had made such a splash.

Kids loved Goldie.

Parents and social media did, too.

There were memes upon memes, Goldie had been booked for parties and fundraisers and a wine trolley event in the North Bay.

A glittering giant poop on a *wine trolley*.

How? Why?

All because Kacee had taken some pictures, rocked out to *Hand Clap*, and…was glittering…and giant…

Sigh.

The rehabbed nugget had come, and they'd tried it during one game…

Well, for one period of one game because the crowd had booed so much when Kacee had debuted the corrected costume (and had thrown popcorn and—in one douche canoe move—had dumped a beer on her) that they'd changed back to #GlitteryGoldieGuano (see what she did there with the hashtag? Wink. Wink. Though reasonably, she couldn't take credit for it. The fans were behind adding the "ie").

Goldie, the giant poop, was there to stay.

"The Miner or Goldie aside," Fanny murmured. "We weren't laughing *at* you. We were laughing because Kay had told us *every single time* we told him he should ask you out, that you weren't interested. That you didn't like him. That you would never agree to go out with him."

"I hadn't planned to," Scar admitted.

Mandy smiled. "Girl, I feel you on that, but all my plans went out the window, and now two kids later, I still have my hockey player."

A warm feeling coiled in Scar's stomach.

She wanted that with Kaydon.

The kids. The happy ending.

"I got the vibe from you," Mandy told her. "The I'm-interested-but-I'm-scared vibe." A self-deprecating smile. "Want to tell me how I'm an expert in that particular set of feelings?"

"Or how *I* do?" Fanny added softly.

Mandy nodded, acknowledging that before she moved on. "But Kaydon was convinced you didn't like him, and he wouldn't listen when we told him otherwise. When we told him to ask you out. When we encouraged—"

"Strongly," Fanny said.

"Strongly," Mandy agreed. "Him to make a move." A sigh as she clasped her hands to her chest. "So, apparently he eventually did, but because you two were so damned secretive, we didn't get to play matchmaker."

"And seriously! That was the worst part." Fanny huffed. "I was ready for my turn to be in on the gossip."

Mandy made a face. "True. We did have to wait and watch, and here we thought we had the inside information, the inside track, but you never let on that you were together." A knowing look.

"I didn't want…" She trailed off.

They waited.

"I didn't want anyone to think I wasn't good enough for him."

Mandy wrapped her arm around Scar's shoulders. "I'm sorry that I gave you the impression that I would ever think that. You're kind and smart and funny. You bend over backward for everyone else."

Fanny repeated the action on the other side. "You're beautiful"—a tap to her chest, just above her heart—"in here"—one to her temple—"*and* here. We're lucky to have you with the Gold and even luckier to have you as a friend."

Scar sighed. "The drama, the disasters that seem to happen —" She shook her head. "Hell, just look at Goldie. It was one of *my* projects and—"

"The entire Twitterverse is talking about it? *And* the Gold?" Mandy asked dryly.

"Yeah, Scar," Fanny said dryly. "All that free publicity is tough, and management sure is hating it."

"It's a joke."

Fanny bumped her lightly. "And one we're all aware of. It's a good thing for the team. *You're* a good thing for the team, for Kaydon, for *us.*"

She sniffed and, only half-joking, said, "You like Charlie better."

Fanny laughed. "Hell no. The man is a terrible shopper." She turned, hugged Scar tight. "I love you, goofball, you *and* your nutty brother who for some reason loves reality TV but doesn't appreciate the home goods aisles at Target. But most of all, you're family, and I don't want you to ever think that I'm not on your side."

"Even if I pick the quote-unquote *wrong* couple on *Dancing with the Stars?*"

Fanny made a face. "Even then—though I *will* complain about it."

"That was never in doubt," Scar said dryly.

Quiet fell.

Not tense this time.

But contemplative.

"I didn't think…" Scar sighed. "I didn't think that I'd ever be anything but a disappointment. To my family. To my friends. To my…employer. To…everyone." Mandy made a noise of protest but didn't otherwise interrupt. "But I'm working on seeing myself as more. I think—" She made a face. "I think I'm mostly there. Six months ago, I would have buried this, would have plastered it over and pretended I hadn't gotten my feelings hurt—all while using it as evidence that, see? I was right. I *am* a disappointment."

"So, you've taken a huge step," Mandy said. "And maybe next time, you'll march right into that locker room and put us in our places."

Scar paused, considered that. Then grinned because, "Damn right, I will."

"I love you," Fanny blurted, hugging her tight.

"I-I love you, too," she whispered, and threw her arm around Mandy, "and you, too. I love you both."

They sat there for a minute, arms around each other, quiet and soaking in the sap.

Then Mandy tugged Scar to her feet, repeated the process with Fanny. "As much as I love you both," she said. "I have *got* to get this outfit picked out and get home to feed the babies. Otherwise, I will never make it on this date night."

"You know you'd already be done if you just bought the dress Scar and I picked out," Fanny cajoled.

Mandy made a face. "It's too sexy, and I'm too fat and…" She trailed off, looked woefully at the racks.

Scar looked to Fanny, cut off Mandy. "All right then." She clapped her hands together and signaled them forward. "Operation Knock Blane's Socks Off is reconvened."

Fanny nodded fiercely. "Awaiting your orders, Captain."

They fist-bumped.

Then immediately moved forward and picked the ugliest items they could find, loading them into their arms and bringing them over to their friend.

Mandy took one look at the dresses they'd selected and sighed. "Okay. You win. I'll get the dress."

"*And* the jacket?" Fanny pressed.

A nod. "And the jacket."

"And shoes and earrings and new lingerie?" Scar asked.

A frown. "I—"

"You're the complete package, Mandy," Scar said. "Now act like it."

Mandy's mouth turned up, and she shook her head. "Now, how can I ignore good advice like that?"

"You can't," Fanny pointed out.

They laughed…and then they headed to the lingerie section.

And Scar went, feeling a thousand pounds lighter.

Because she'd done it.

She was doing it.

Fuck disappointments. This, living like *this*, was…exceeding her wildest expectations.

CHAPTER THIRTY

Kaydon

THE BUZZER HAD GONE.

The rink had emptied out.

Press and post-game cooldowns were complete.

Showers had been taken.

His family was waiting.

Scar had gone to the airport to pick up Charlie and would be meeting him at his parents' house for a BBQ, since the game had started at noon.

It was four now, they had the next day off, and though it was going to kill him to not be able to partake of his mom's sweet corn casserole (it was—sadly—not a Cheat Day), he was still excited to introduce Scar to his family.

And Charlie.

So, he'd stick to the rice and tofu his dad was gainfully preparing, fill up on greens and water, and have the one beer he was allowed.

And he wouldn't be mopey.

Because Scar was coming.

Grinning, he finished toweling off, got dressed, and hauled

ass outside of the locker room, even while he ignored the calls of, "Bye, Kitten!"

Or rather, instead of ignoring, he flipped the room the bird and then went on his merry way.

His family was waiting on the concourse, so he went up to find them, hopping in an elevator, riding it up, and—

"Kaydon!"

His youngest sister, Cami, threw her arms around him. "Hey, kiddo," he said, hugging her back. "How's school?"

She was in the middle of her senior year of high school. "Good."

"You heard back from any colleges yet?"

A shake of her head. "It's too early."

"Well, let me know as soon as you do, okay?"

"I will."

He hugged her one more time and then turned to greet the rest of his family. His older brother Robert was there, along with his middle brother, Cane. His younger brother and sister—twins, because good on his parents—Reese and Blair, respectively, were off at college. His sister, Blair, was killing it at Northwestern, playing hockey and acing classes. Reese was focusing on his art and was going to school in New York City.

Cane and Robert had both stayed in Minnesota and helped his parents at their lumber company.

And since his mom and dad were more than ready to retire to summer and never deal with the snow again, Kaydon knew it wouldn't be too long before his brothers took it over.

"Mom," he said, when she wrapped her arms around him. "How are you?"

"Me?" she asked, hugging him tight for a second before patting him on the shoulder. "I'm fine. How are you? How's the knee? Where's Scar and Charlie? And—oh! I made two pans of casserole. Do you think that will be enough? We can always stop by the store and—"

"Mom," he said gently, kissing her on the forehead, "Scar is picking up Charlie at the airport. She texted and said his flight is delayed, so they'll be there as soon as they can. My knee is fine. I'm fantastic. And two pans is definitely enough."

Turning, he greeted everyone else, exchanged the requisite hugs and handshakes and fist-bumps, then as everyone started walking to his parents' car, he bent and whispered in his mom's ear. "This is for you." He handed her the bag that Scar had put together. "From Scar."

"A present?" she exclaimed. "For me?"

He nodded, wrapped his arm around her, and said, "Scar wanted to give it to you herself, but then she got embarrassed and second-guessed herself." He guided them out the door. "She left it at home"—he did air quotes—"by accident. But luckily, I remembered it."

His mom glanced up at him.

He winked.

She grinned.

"Why would she be embarrassed?"

He nodded at the bag. "Look inside."

His mom pulled the tissue paper to the side, and then she gasped, "She *didn't*."

"She did," he confirmed. "She found your shelf at my place, realized you two read the same books. So, she got you the rest of the series, including an advanced copy of the one that's coming out next month."

"How?"

They moved to the car, unlocked the doors, and everyone got in except him and his mom.

He shrugged. "Scar called in a favor from a connection she had. They sent it, and then she added a few of her favorites that she wasn't sure you'd read."

His mom pulled out the top book on the stack, the advanced copy, and flipped open the cover. "Oh my God, and it's signed, too?"

"That's all Scar."

Carefully setting the books down, his mom rose on tiptoe, kissed his cheek. "I love her." A smile. "I mean, I would *already* love her because she's put that look in your eyes, but this…this is such a sweet gesture, and I can't believe that she thought to do it."

"She's like that," he murmured. "Thinking of everyone else."

A pat to his cheek. "Then you'd better make sure that you think of *her* first, okay?"

That wouldn't be a problem, but he knew better than to argue. "Okay, Mom." He opened her door, and she started to climb into the passenger's seat. "Mom?"

She paused. "Yeah, honey?"

"What look do I have in my eyes?"

His mom smiled. "The same one your father wears when he looks at me."

———

THE DOORBELL RANG, and he had to use his boxing out skills —thanks hockey—to beat his family to the door.

"It's supposed to be a backyard barbecue," he muttered, bumping Cami to the side. "Which means you're supposed to be in the *back yard.*"

"Not until we meet Scarlett," Cami said, trying to squeeze by him.

"Scar," he reminded. "She prefers to be called Scar, remember?"

"Right. Scar." Cami reached for the doorknob.

"Cami," his mom said. "Back yard."

It was in that tone—the *Mom* Tone. Which meant that Cami couldn't ignore it.

Huffing, she went into the back yard, Robert and Cane following her, muttering about yards and just trying to be polite.

His mom kissed his cheek. "Bring her back when's she's ready, okay?"

"Okay," he said, nodding.

She turned, made her way back into the kitchen.

Smiling, Kay reached for the knob, tugged open the door, and realized...

He should have looked through the peephole first.

CHAPTER THIRTY-ONE

Scar

SHE AND CHARLIE were jamming to their road trip playlist.

Vanilla Ice, Boyz II Men, Backstreet Boys, Britney, Gaga, Maroon 5, Credence Clearwater, Huey Lewis and the News, The Beach Boys, The Rolling Stones, Nirvana.

She knew it wouldn't be hard to tell who'd added which songs.

She knew it would surprise people how much hers and her brother's eclectic taste in music overlapped.

Pretty much the only song she'd added that he couldn't stand was *Ice, Ice Baby*.

The only song *she* couldn't stand was *Barbara Ann*—too many baba's in that for her taste.

Their compatible (albeit strange) musical tastes meant they sang a lot, talked a little, and zipped through the miles between the airport and Kaydon's parents' house.

All that singing also meant that she didn't have time to be nervous.

Or not *too* nervous, anyway.

Because singing...and because she'd promised herself that

she wasn't doing this anymore. She was done with the doubt, the disappointment.

She had Kaydon and Charlie and her friends and her work.

And she didn't bring drama.

She was herself, and that was pretty damned good.

Nodding—though luckily it went along with *(I Can't Get No) Satisfaction*—she glanced at her phone to check the final turn and saw that Kaydon had texted. Well, they were a half-mile away. She'd check it when they got there.

She signaled, went around the corner, and began checking house numbers.

"Sixty-six," she muttered. "Sixty-eight. *Seventy.* There." She pulled into an opening, noted that there were a lot of vehicles near the house. Though, she supposed with six siblings there were bound to be a lot of cars around.

But only four were supposed to be there tonight.

Hmm.

She shrugged.

Maybe they'd changed their minds, or maybe they decided to have some friends over. Either way—she shrugged—there would be people there, she would be herself, and all would be fine. It would all be—

She frowned as they walked by a car with a license plate for Ohio.

That was her home state.

And it looked like a rental.

Weird.

"Come on," Charlie said, snagging her arm. "I need some of whatever has made that delicious smell in my belly."

Smiling, she let him drag her up to the front door and ring the bell.

There were footsteps inside, a long pause, and then the door opened…

Charlie stepped into hell, Scar right behind him.

"Fuck," Charlie muttered. "Scar, get back in the car."

Scar blinked at his tone, fear rippling through her. "What—?"

She leaned around him, caught a glance of the entryway that was filled with people, and finally understood the meaning of the sentiment *I can't believe my eyes.*

Because...how?

Her *parents* were in the entry, standing in the opening of what looked to be a perfectly nice living room—except for the fact that it was marred by *her parents.* Kaydon's mom was moving back to stand at Kaydon's side, concern on her face, her hands wrinkling the floral pattern of her apron. His dad was at his other shoulder, fury in his eyes, fury that was mirrored by the faces of who she assumed were his siblings, stacked three deep in the hall, a glass door showing a deck and lush green trees behind them.

Oak floors, pale yellow paint, family pictures crammed on every wall and flat surface.

Shoes by the front door, tucked beneath a bench, hooks with coats, cream cabinets with bright blue pulls, and knobs through the other doorway.

Scar tried to commit every detail to memory.

Before it was ruined.

No...not ruined. It couldn't be ruined.

Could it?

She took in faces. Kaydon's apoplectic one. His siblings and father's furious one. His mother's concerned one.

No smiles.

All serious.

All *seriously* fucked up because of two people in the fucking hallway who had absolutely no reason to be there.

"Scarlett darling," her mother said, trying sweet as honey on for a change (probably because of their audience). "It's been too long."

"Not long enough," Charlie muttered.

"Come give your mommy a hug," she said, ignoring her son's comment.

And…what?

She'd never been a mom, let alone a *mommy*, and Scar wasn't going anywhere near those claws.

"You should leave," Kaydon said.

Ignoring him, her mom took a step toward Charlie and Scar. "I missed my babies. I—" She reached out like she was going to hug them, but Charlie moved, angling his body so he was between her and their mom, putting his arm out to stop the motion so that their mom hugged it instead of them.

"Charlie," she snapped, losing the veneer for a moment. "I didn't give you permission to be here."

"Charlie, Scar, honey," Kaydon said. "Come here."

Charlie had frozen at the tone—the one that had always begun the onslaught, the yelling and belittling, the threats. They all had different ways of dealing with it. Charlie's was to get quiet, to retreat, to shut everything down so that it didn't hurt so much.

Scar—well, it was obvious that Scar had run, or tried to, anyway, and then internalized all of that bullshit.

However, even though her brother had frozen, Kaydon's words unstuck him.

He moved toward the love of her life, and when he got near enough, Scar didn't miss that Kaydon's mom shifted closer.

Protective.

Like her son.

Unlike the woman sneering at her son she'd never accepted because he was different, and putting on a show like she loved her daughter, even though that had never been true. Because Scar wasn't perfect. Because Scar wasn't Heath.

Because Scar wasn't her mother.

"Sweetcheeks," Kaydon murmured. "*Baby*, come here."

Scar glanced at him and then shook her head.

This had to end now. She needed to do this.

"I'm not you," she whispered.

Her mom had started to open her mouth, no doubt to try *honey* back on for size, to try and manipulate the situation to her benefit.

And Scar, unfortunately, thought she knew what it was.

"What?" her mother asked, brows drawing together.

"I'm *not* you," Scar repeated, louder this time. "I'm not the type of woman who will realize who her daughter is dating and track down his family—"

"We didn't track them down."

Scar glanced around the room, her brows raised. "Am I missing the part where you were invited?" Her eyes caught on Kaydon's mom's, and the other woman nodded encouragingly, gave her the strength to keep finding her words.

Especially when her mother said, "Charlie did."

Charlie startled. "You have lost your mind."

"He did. He put it on Facebook that he was flying out here. Put it right where anyone could see it, and we were in the neighborhood and knew you'd want us to visit and—"

"You thought you'd show up because you recognized Kaydon from the run-in at our house and realized who he was and that he has money, and you thought that you'd come here and somehow manipulate him into giving you some?"

"That's absurd."

But her tone was off, her acting skills were faltering.

No Oscars would be going her way.

She seemed to realize that, and quickly turned to Scar's dad, who was, as usual on his phone. It was either play Good Cop or on the cell, there was no in-between. "Tell them, Mike," her mom said. "Tell them Charlie put it—"

"We were in the neighborhood," her dad said, barely glancing up.

Oh my God.

This was...horrific.

"Kaydon is not going to give you any money," Scar said,

straightening her shoulders. "Not now. Not ever. It's his money, and I will make sure that I sign a prenuptial agreement that gives me *nothing*." She stepped closer, jabbed a finger in her mom's direction. "Because I will do anything to make sure that you never get to touch it. You ruined my childhood, ruined Charlie and Heath's, too. You're selfish, inconsiderate, abusive, and downright *mean*."

"Well, I—" her mom sputtered.

Scar had let loose, and there wasn't any stopping, not at that moment. "And if you want something, want *anything*, you should be pleased that you have the knowledge that you've alienated and hurt and fucked with the three people you were supposed to love beyond measure." Scar started clapping. "So congrats, Mom. You may not get an Oscar for acting like Mom of the Year, but you certainly could get one for being the Douchebag of the Decade."

She kept on clapping.

It was loud in the quiet hall, loud in the stunned silence of her parents, loud when Kaydon's family stood so still.

But she kept going.

For all the times her mom had been mean to Heath, cruel to Charlie, horrible to her.

For all the times the manipulation had worked, and Scar had given in.

For all the times Scar had thought *she* wasn't worthy, all the disappointments, the pain, the tears.

And then...

Kaydon's mom began clapping.

A slow *clap-clap* that connected with Scar's, that added to the volume, that sucked the power away from her parents, from her mother who played the aggressor and her father who was just as bad because he was on the sidelines, watching it happen, and then happily allowing himself to be subbed in.

"Craphead of the Century," came a female voice, a head

popping up, a wide smile on her lips, her hair bouncing as she joined in on the clapping.

"Craphead?" one of Kaydon's brothers—which one, she didn't know because they hadn't had a chance to be introduced yet *(thanks, Mom!)*—said.

Cami—his youngest sister was Cami—shrugged, still clapping. "It was either that or cu—"

"Whoa!" the other brother exclaimed. "Craphead is good. Craphead is perfect." He joined in on the clapping. His brother following suit. Kaydon's dad barely a heartbeat after that.

Kaydon grinned at her, and said, "Motherfucker of the Millennium."

That got him a look from his mom, but when he started clapping, Charlie a moment behind him, it transformed into begrudging approval.

Meanwhile, her mom was sputtering, looking around, her cheeks crimson, her shoulders slowly slumping inward. Maybe Scar should feel bad for humiliating her. After all, she didn't want to be like her. But try as she might, she couldn't summon the feeling.

"So, please, Mom," she said. "Please just fuck right off and leave me to my life. Quit trying to suck out my happiness because you're so goddamned miserable."

The clapping died down.

Her mom looked to her father, searching his face as though he'd intervene.

He didn't, of course.

The only one to belittle in that moment was his partner in crime.

Scar sighed and said, "I will never, *ever* welcome you back into my life. *Charlie* will never either. We're done, and I don't ever want to see either of you again."

Her mother tried one more time—because *of course* she did. "I've never been spoken to like—"

"I know," Scar interrupted quietly. "And it was far overdue."

Silence.

Then, "Here." Kaydon extended a wad of bills. "Gas money for you to—as Scar so eloquently put it—fuck right off out of here."

Like a dog to a bone, her dad put his cell away, snagged the money, and dragged her mom out the front door.

"How much was that?" she asked after he closed and locked the door behind them.

Kaydon cupped her face gently, pressed a soft kiss to her lips. "Sixteen dollars."

She startled then smiled. "God, I love you."

He bent, murmured in her ear, "You were magnificent."

She smiled. "I don't know what came over me, but I'm damned happy it did."

"Me, too." He tugged her hair, kissed her lightly, then said, "Prenuptial agreement?"

Her mind rewound to that moment, skidded to a halt. "I—"

"I accept," he teased, nipping at her earlobe. "As soon as you buy me a ring, I'm all yours."

She groaned, buried her face in his chest, and sighed. "I... probably just made the worst impression ever on your folks."

He pulled back enough so that she had to lift her head, so that she had to meet his eyes. "If they have one iota of sense—which I know they do—then they will agree with me." He wove his fingers into her hair, kissed her until her heart galloped in her chest. "Because you were fucking fantastic, sweetcheeks."

Scar took a breath, smiled, and because she finally, *finally* could do it, nodded.

Then said, "Yeah, yeah I was."

Fuck disappointments.

She'd take fantastic any day of the week.

EPILOGUE

Kaydon, the next day

"You know this was a mistake, right?" his dad said, looking over at Scar.

"Best mistake of my life," he replied, holding the door as his mom, who'd linked arms with Scar, breezed into the bookstore.

His dad clapped him on the shoulder. "Damned right it is, son. Damned right it is."

They followed in the wake of the women, pursuing the thriller section while the women disappeared to God knew where.

"I'm just saying," his dad murmured as he glanced at the back cover of a popular book, "you're going to be paying through the nose in overweight luggage."

"Well, good thing I've got that big contract and all that money."

His dad nudged him then glanced at the inside of the cover to the flap that showed the price for the hardcover. And promptly set it down. "That you used to pay off your mom's and my house *and* the business loan *and* your siblings' tuition?"

Kaydon shrugged. "I have it. You all needed it. God knows

I'm not hurting for it. I have a nice house, good clothes, food, and a woman who loves me." He picked up the book his dad had set down, put it in the stack to buy. "I'm happy, and that's all I can ask for."

"I'm happy for you," his dad said, discarding another book.

Which Kay picked up.

"And that's all I can ask for as a dad." A beat. "And I'm fucking proud of you, son."

Kaydon let that wash over him, allowed the warm words to fill him up. So lucky. He was so fucking lucky to have the parents he did. "Dad?"

"Yeah?" he asked, discarding a third book which Kaydon grabbed.

"Thanks for being you."

His dad froze, his gaze on the book he'd been studying for a long moment. Then he lifted his head, and Kay's throat got tight when he saw the dampness in his dad's eyes.

He forced what he needed to say out, wanted to make sure his dad—who'd taken Charlie into the back yard the night before, got him working on the grill and talked to him about nothing important, except that it would distract him from what had happened. Who'd then rescued Scar from the kitchen and his mom's task mastering of peeling potatoes and cutting the kernels off corncobs (a distraction, but not the one Kay had wanted her to have after that scene). Who'd given her a hard seltzer and ordered her to tell him all about her job.

Who'd always put his family first no matter what, not needing the clear example they'd been given in the hall, the shittiness exhibited by Scar's parents.

Who'd made certain that Scar and Charlie already knew they were family, too.

Yeah, he'd won the lottery jackpot with his parents.

He'd known it before.

He especially knew it now.

After a few seltzers, Scar and his mom had talked books. By

then, Scar had relaxed enough to talk to Cane and Robert about the business, Cami about school.

Because of his parents. Because of his family.

Because of…her.

Because she was a fucking beast…who was coming around the corner with a stack of books a body-builder should be carrying in her arms. She spotted him. "Oh hi, baby," she said. "I just need to go back and grab one more—"

His dad chuckled.

Kay snagged the stack, added it to the four books his dad had discarded after checking the prices, and asked, "Don't you have enough?"

She whirled, her ponytail flying behind her. "Don't you dare ask that question, Mr. Library. There is no such thing as enough books."

She flounced off.

His dad grinned. "Best mistake."

Kaydon chuckled. "Best mistake."

They trailed her over to the case, and to his surprise, it wasn't the romance section.

She snagged a book off the shelf, held it up. *Rustic Interiors: Farmhouse Chic.* "I'm doing it," she said. "I've made a decision, and I've figured out what I want to do for the rest of the rooms."

He winced.

Her face fell. "What?" she asked. "You don't like it?"

"It's not that," he hedged.

She set the book down. "You don't like—"

"Stop," he said and placed the books on the carpet, snagged the farmhouse chic one, and put it on her stack. "If that's what you want, sweetcheeks, that's what you'll have. It's just—" He pulled out his phone, knowing it would be easier to just show her. "You know the reason Charlie had to fly out super early this morning?"

"He had a job interview."

Kay shook his head as he hit the FaceTime button. "No, sweetcheeks, he didn't."

Charlie picked up on the third ring, and noise blared through the speakers, music and saws and drills and so many people talking. "Hey, Kay. I just got here, and everything's underway," Charlie shouted.

"What's going on?" Scar whispered.

He brought her close, nodded at the screen.

"That's my house."

"Scar?" Charlie frowned. "You're not supposed—"

"Cat's out of the bag, man," Kay told him.

A beat. Then, "Do you want to see it?"

"See *what?*" she asked, her eyes going from the screen to Kaydon.

"Mandy and Fanny wanted to do something for you. They found your secret Pinterest board"—which probably meant they'd hacked into her phone somehow because those two never let a small thing like security protocols get in their way— "and they arranged a designer, a construction crew, and a foreman—"

He nodded toward the phone, toward Charlie.

"The crew is supposed to have everything done by the time that we get back from the road trip."

"That's why Charlie could only fly in for the day?"

Kay nodded again.

"Oh, my God," she breathed. "But the money—"

"The team took up a collection."

Her cheeks flared. "I couldn't—"

"They love you," he said. "And since you wouldn't let anyone but me help with the projects, they decided that they needed to save my energy, and," he added when her flush spread, "that they'd needed to save you from my shoddy work-manship." He shook his head. "A man installs *one* washer wrong, and it leaks all over the floor, and—"

She threw her arms around his neck and kissed him.

Right there in the bookstore.

In front of his dad and her brother and who knew how many books.

Not a dark corner. Not hiding.

In the daylight. In his arms.

The best fucking mistake of his life.

And it somehow got better. Because when she dropped back down onto the soles of her feet, her arms still around him, her books scattered at their feet, she smiled at him—bright and full and without any hint of pain—then said, "About that prenup."

And pulled out a ring.

A pink plastic ring with Hello Kitty's face on it.

And for *that*, he had to kiss her again.

CAUGHT

Charlie

HE WOVE his way through the bowels of the arena, waiting for Fanny or Scar or Kaydon or Mandy.

Or any of the people he wanted to see.

As opposed to the one person he was trying to *avoid* seeing. Ji-Ho.

His ex had taken a transfer and was now working in the San Francisco office, and…he was at the Gold game that evening.

In the company box.

Charlie hadn't been there, thankfully, even though he worked for the same company, the same branch. Even though he'd worked with Ji-Ho in Korea—

Love. A broken heart. Despair. Now…alone. So *fucking* alone.

Needless to say, he'd been avoiding Ji-Ho since he'd heard of his ex's transfer.

But that wasn't why he hadn't been in the Steele Technologies box. His sister worked for the Gold, so he usually sat in the team box when he came to catch a game, watching her do her publicist thing, smiling as she mooned over her gorgeous hockey player man...*fiancé?*

He wasn't quite sure where they stood. Kaydon never took off a plastic Hello Kitty ring his sister had proposed with, but Scar wasn't sporting a diamond, and though they'd moved in together, neither of them appeared to be moving toward setting any wedding dates.

It was just...a love fest.

All the time.

His friend—and former date (*one* date, but still)—Fanny, and her husband Brandon. Scar and Kaydon. Mandy and Blane. Brit and Stefan. Coop and Calle. Char and Logan. Dani and Ethan. Mia and—

Well, the point was that there weren't a lot of prospects for a single man on this team.

Even less so when he considered that none of the single men were bi or gay or interested in a semi-scrawny (at least compared to them) redhead bisexual man who'd had his heart broken and had run away like a baby because of it. *And* all the women he knew were paired up.

Because if they were single and interested, he would be *such* a catch, right?

Right.

And yes, that was sarcasm.

So anyway, he'd been sitting on the chair next to Scar, amazed at all the things she did at once and handled with aplomb, and he'd turned, and...

Ji-Ho.

In the next box over.

Charlie had wanted to run, to hide, to pretend he hadn't seen his ex.

But...pride.

So, he had lifted his chin, held his stare steady when their eyes had locked, and...he'd pretended that his heart wasn't still cracked.

Still shattered.

It wouldn't have worked out. He knew that now. But, fuck, he'd moved halfway around the world to be closer to the man he'd met at a conference, a man he'd thought might be something permanent, and they'd ended up…

As a disaster.

He'd moved home.

Now Ji-Ho was here. *Why* was he here?

Charlie wasn't about to find out. Not when the man had cheated on him. Not when he'd sabotaged Charlie's work. Not when…he hadn't treated Charlie's heart with the same care every couple in this strange cornucopia of happy endings treated their partners' hearts.

He wanted *that*.

Care.

To receive. To give.

And he deserved it.

"*I* deserve it," he whispered, pushing through the door to a room that was usually empty, intending to take a moment to get that sentiment through his thick, still-sort-of-pining-for-Ji-Ho-even-though-that-was-fucking-stupid-because-Ji-Ho-was-a-creep skull.

However, instead of making his way through the door, he collided with something firm and huge…

And gold.

No *Gold*. As in, Goldie.

The #GlitteryGoldieGuano.

The giant poop-shaped mascot that had somehow become—much to Scar's chagrin—a fan-favorite. With their collision, the poop—well, the costume performer—tipped over backward, landing with an *oof* that made Charlie cringe and rush forward, kneeling at the glittering dump's side.

The triangular piece at the top had popped off, rolled across the room.

"Are you oka—"

His words froze in his throat. His heart seized.

Because the top of that giant golden poop had fallen off and revealed…

The most beautiful woman he'd ever seen.

———

CHARLIE'S STORY is coming February 1st, 2022. Preorder your copy at https://books2read.com/caughtef/

A GOLD CHRISTMAS

Surprise! Brit and Stefan are returning with plenty of Christmas cheer! Or…maybe Christmas *grinchness*…

Either way, their *after* their happily-ever-after is sure to be full of flannel, sparkle, and peppermint hot cocoa!

Preorder your copy at www.books2read.com/AGoldXmas and enjoy beginning November 9th, 2021!

———

Hate missing Elise's new releases? Love contests, exclusive excerpts and giveaways?

Then signup for Elise's newsletter here!

http://eepurl.com/bdnmEj

———

And join Elise's fan group, the Fabinators (https://www.facebook.com/groups/fabinators) for insider information, sneak peaks at new releases, and fun freebies! Hope to see you there!

———

GOLD HOCKEY SERIES

Blocked

Backhand

Boarding

Benched

Breakaway

Breakout

Checked

Coasting

Centered

Charging

Caged

Crashed

Cycled

A Gold Christmas

Caught

ALSO BY ELISE FABER

Billionaire's Club **(all stand alone)**

Bad Night Stand

Bad Breakup

Bad Husband

Bad Hookup

Bad Divorce

Bad Fiancé

Bad Boyfriend

Bad Blind Date

Bad Wedding

Bad Engagement

Bad Bridesmaid

Bad Swipe

Bad Girlfriend

Bad Best Friend

Gold Hockey **(all stand alone)**

Blocked

Backhand

Boarding

Benched

Breakaway

Breakout

Checked

Coasting

Centered

Charging

Caged

Crashed

Cycled

Caught

Breakers Hockey **(all stand alone)**

Broken

Boldly

Breathless

KTS Series

Riding The Edge

Crossing The Line

Leveling The Field

Scorching The Earth

Love, Action, Camera (all stand alone)

Dotted Line

Action Shot

Close-Up

End Scene

Meet Cute

Love After Midnight **(all stand alone)**

Rum And Notes

Virgin Daiquiri

On The Rocks

Sex On The Seats

Life Sucks Series **(all stand alone)**

Train Wreck

Hot Mess

Dumpster Fire

Clusterf*@k

FUBAR

Roosevelt Ranch Series (all stand alone, series complete)

Disaster at Roosevelt Ranch

Heartbreak at Roosevelt Ranch

Collision at Roosevelt Ranch

Regret at Roosevelt Ranch

Desire at Roosevelt Ranch

Phoenix Series (read in order)

Phoenix Rising

Dark Phoenix

Phoenix Freed

Phoenix: LexTal Chronicles (rereleasing soon, stand alone, Phoenix world)

From Ashes

In Flames

To Smoke

ABOUT THE AUTHOR

USA Today bestselling author, Elise Faber, loves chocolate, Star Wars, Harry Potter, and hockey (the order depending on the day and how well her team -- the Sharks! -- are playing). She and her husband also play as much hockey as they can squeeze into their schedules, so much so that their typical date night is spent on the ice. Elise changes her hair color more often than some people change their socks, loves sparkly things, and is the mom to two exuberant boys. She lives in Northern California. Connect with her in her Facebook group, the Fabinators or find more information about her books at www.elisefaber.com.

f facebook.com/elisefaberauthor
a amazon.com/author/elisefaber
BB bookbub.com/profile/elise-faber
instagram.com/elisefaber
g goodreads.com/elisefaber
pinterest.com/elisefaberwrite

Made in the USA
Middletown, DE
26 January 2022